Into the Abyss

Into the Abyss

Ravi Singh

Matador
Unit E2 Airfield Business Park,
Harrison Road, Market Harborough,
Leicestershire. LE16 7UL
Tel: 0116 279 2299
Email: books@troubador.co.uk
Web: www.troubador.co.uk/matador
Twitter: @matadorbooks

ISBN 978-1-80514-032-0

British Library Cataloguing in Publication Data.
A catalogue record for this book is available from the British Library.

Printed and bound by CPI Group (UK) Ltd, Croydon, CR0 4YY
Typeset in 11pt Adobe Garamond Pro by Troubador Publishing Ltd, Leicester, UK

Matador is an imprint of Troubador Publishing Ltd

For

Rhonda

Our beautiful sister
In our hearts
You will live forever

Contents

Preface

What I am today is not by coincidence, why I have decided, and what I am writing about, correspondingly. It is the result of something that drove me for many years, compelled I was, I am still, wanting to understand conflict. Why people kill?

What drives us? What motivates us to kill each other, even neighbours? Someone, you once considered as a brother or a sister. If I could just find out why, I could help, thought I could be a peace maker.

How does he do it? I thought about Dr Saeb Erekat, the Palestinian negotiator. I would be in awe and wonder, determined I was to be just like him, an international negotiator. Part of the solution, the idea, the thought, the position, the role, any young man's dream, glamorous. A mediator became, but, would not be like him. What would it take to rise to such a level? The few that knows, but guess, it is you, those who know. Since, I do not live in a conflict zone. How could I then fulfil such a role?

Educated I was in law, as well international, it was intentional. Had to expand my knowledge, so I embarked on inter-state relations. Knew, I did not make a mistake, I was fascinated by it, everything made sense. The puzzle in my mind, pieced together, soon to discover, a huge piece was missing, however. How can we explain what is currently happening? Not again, war among nations, but inside the borders, amongst those within. My PhD embarked to answer this question, at the very start, it was loaded with problems.

My first attempt, how to resolve the intractable. I thought conflict resolution, from Colombia, Jaffna, to the streets of Ramallah, Jerusalem. Naivety, fool I was thinking, could be done so easily. Could not be done before, why now? Good intentions, does not make it happen. My supervisor did not make it easy, part of the problem, so confused she was, never understood the question. If we can make them understand, the belligerents, that is, if they would only sit and listen, they could work out things, as the novice would think. Two years would pass, I would realise, people do settle and resolve their differences, but only at the brink. Futile this effort, defending such a thesis, might be laughed out the room, I thought, I cannot present this.

The second attempt, was much more promising, how to stop conflicts, or prevent them from escalating. The effort to save the innocents, the 'Responsibility to Protect' was all we needed. Would seem only a bargaining chip though, and it has proven. Realising, it all came down to politics, the highest. On the Security Council, the hard heads that knock and block, it cannot work out, I thought. What drove Intervention in Libya, but not in Syria? It was clear, if you have friends, you can literally get away with murder. Again stomped, the Security Council I realised, was the 'main' problem. Humanitarian Intervention, Armed, the peacekeepers turned peace-makers, the Rapid Reaction Force would never happen.

My third and final attempt, it made a lot more sense.

We must use diplomacy to stop what is presently. A political solution if you will, since all else has failed, regrettably. Some things must run its course, conflicts included. If we only knew before, we would never let it happen. It became very clear, we must go back to the source of the problem. *We must prevent conflicts from ever happening.* Conflict prevention and peace building, they are one and the same, the only difference is, one is less expensive, much, much less. With prevention, you do not have to deal with destruction, there is no need to rebuild, nor health care expensive. There is no loss of life, not even traumatised children, no need for emergency education.

This is it then, I was sold, this would be my new goal. By now qualified in Conflictology, my whole life has lived and studied. The details would specialise, armed conflict with focus on intra-state. Could not at this point say it all happened, but, in some ways it did. I have worked as a conflict analyst, made some trips, given advice, conflict sensitive. Did not have the credentials of a humanitarian, though in my heart, I am one, I felt it. Been told many times, you can only deal with crisis. A good contract could not secure, I was unable to convince. I have never brought food, livelihood, those in need secure. Never been a doctor MSF, drilled wells, provide water or, build shelter for the displaced poor. Peace and conflict, all I know. I did not give up, though.

If only, short term jobs secure, one, a few weeks, two months, three. It is better I thought, balance my life, I can still be there for my family. If I could just work, long enough, help as much as I could, then get back home. But, it would never be sufficient, to make a real difference. Those of us, what we go through? The many friends I have known, have sacrificed their family, to save the many. Understand, if they could only, they are also part of the solution, the family support, would help prop you up. It is never that easy, for those of us who see, when we try to realise our destiny.

As many knows. Those cannot, teach, sometimes a choice, sometimes not. Out of the question in my case, would not enjoy such a privilege. Always hands on, since I cannot anymore, live it. I have decided on the next best thing, I would write about it. It has always been my intention, that one day, I would write about conflict. Hopefully soon, the opportunity awaited, then came Covid, unexpected. Not the Kid we know, but a pandemic. Many will be lost, until we figure it out, sadly, but, much more would lose their jobs, the economy. Artificial, unsustainable, the bubbles that burst, the businesses questionable. Not their fault, the innocents pay, in more ways than one, income gone, at home with children, must now stay. They must find a way, ingenuity, some will succeed. The millions will plead, turn to the state, does not have, and cannot abate.

Needless to say, I suffered the same fate, an unpredictable field, the result of my dream. Will suffer, like all the others, future unclear, seems like I am going nowhere. At least, not in a hurry. What was spent before, understanding conflict and building peace? Would now have to go to humanitarian relief. Precedence it takes, of course it does, but what happens when governments get involved. People that is, those believe in politics, tribalism and race. Who will they first, give? Who gets what, remains? The conflict results, back to square one, try to figure out, how this came about?

I could continue, go on and on, but would stray from the point. My task, my main objective, why I decided to write this book, contained in this here, preface. For there are two points to understand. One, why I decided to write this book, the other, how I chose my subject. First, I wanted all who venture, to understand conflict, as do I, and, as I do. Problematic indeed, most would not come to terms. How can I explain? Those, would not have the stomach, if brutally put, for that which is plain? I could somehow try, in the form of a story, academically inclined, I would now have to think creatively. My readers would then connect, if said eloquently. Perhaps would acknowledge, and understand, this is what I hope for, envisage.

Second, my subject, why I decided to write about The Congo, Democratic Republic. It would be wrong, an understatement, to say that only a few cares, it is clear, very few understands, only. The depth and intricacies of this conflict has occupied my thoughts, my mind for a very long time. Knew that I, 'must try to explain it'. I have read hundreds of books on conflict, many about the Republic. Would form my opinion, only at the very last. With you, the time has now come to impart.

Ravi Singh.

Note

Empathy, it is what guided me, as I wrote this book. Could not venture outside these shores, as the pandemic, hold it took. Our borders have been shut, from the very start, I could not travel to conduct research. What to do, I was almost lost, should I give up? Or give my best shot? If I can go, be there, there is so much more I will know. Talk to the people, smell the air, walk the same ground, the sense stronger, feelings they share. Should I not try? This is what I do, put myself in another's shoe. Try as I have, an academic have not found, substantiate, proof read, a great disconnect I feel. What if I am wrong? With some of my assertions, or with my conclusion. Would I be forgiven? Since, this is not exactly, a work of fiction.

It cannot sink me. The pandemic disrupted, it has already. What am I to do, but go bravely, fearlessly? Cannot also, would never allow it to take 'this' from me.

Ravi Singh
June twenty third, 2021.

"The faculty to think objectively is reason; the emotional attitude behind reason is that of humility.

To be objective, to use one's reason, is possible only if one has achieved an attitude of humility, [and] if one has emerged from the dreams of omniscience and omnipotence which one has as a child...

...Love [empathy], being dependent on the relative absence of narcissism, requires the development of humility, objectivity and reason...One's whole life should be devoted to this aim. Humility and objectivity are indivisible...

...I must strive for objectivity in every situation, and become sensitive to the situations where I am not objective...

...I must try to see the difference between my picture of a person and his behaviour, as it is narcissistically distorted, and the person's reality as it exists regardless of my interests, needs and fears".

Erich Fromm, 1956, 109

Introduction

We Close our Eyes

When you take a picture. You may ask nicely, please take the picture of this, my good side. The other side, does not look so good, one thinks. You go on to insist, that you are viewed from a different angle. The cameraman, unable to bear either side, closes his eyes after focusing his shot, and 'click' picture taken. Like two sides of the same coin, there seems to be a choice between one and the other. But it is the same coin, is it not? We may look at ourselves in many ways. And, we honestly believe I think, that this is reality, that we have different persona. But, what is revealed in a picture, framed and put on the wall is really who we are, it is what the world sees. The King of Syria, and his beautiful Queen are decked always in their finest, Italian and French, no less. Oblivious to the fact, that the 'tails' side of their metaphoric coin, are very obvious. Their framed picture is now on the world's wall. Encased, not in polished glass, and gold trimmings, but in 'blood'. I am sorry, Assad might say, please take that picture again, that really, wasn't me.

I watched a documentary about the war in Syria recently. Quite apprehensively, I must say, knowing full well, what was going to come, uncharacteristic for someone who studies conflict. My wife invariably never watches doggie movies, forever anticipating the worst, much to the consternation of my son and I, while we try in vain to get her to look. I know now the reluctance she has, for I to, have experienced this many times. But now, has only come to terms with it.

What makes the events in Syria so troubling? Even to someone like me, who tries very hard to see things dispassionately. But our very 'human nature' apparently precludes, or limits this sense of objectivity. One might conclude therefore, that we are by human nature inherently good, based on our natural inclination of not wanting to see the bad things in the world. But is it that, we are too afraid? *That we might connect with what we are seeing.*

What about those, who presume not to care. Are they inherently bad, or just indifferent then? Surely, they are not bad people, just a different world view. People die, eventually they do, some sooner and some later, is a cynical view, as a doctor friend of mine alluded to. Speaking about the Covid virus, the people who have died, he reasoned, were already sick. They would have died anyway, even, the simple flu had contracted. Why the fuss then, "children can't go to school due to the lockdowns". Having no school age children of his own. I wondered why he would use such an example, he does not have that problem. A Shia gentleman spoke with profound disregard several years ago, while talking about the war in Syria, "Let them kill each other", knowing full well, that it was only one side being killed. Another, a Sunni gentleman, after Nine Eleven, expressed his deep feelings of joy, that it was "good for them", that is, the Americans. By the way, his daughter lives in New York, I wondered if he would felt differently, if his daughter was one of the victims, Allah forbid.

Is this, in a sense, just abandonment? Are we resigned in our thoughts, and our imagination so restricted, that we are unable to see things any differently, than what is to us, presented. I do not, and would never believe that everything is, as it appears, seems. As the portrait of the King and Queen, that hangs so loftily, for the world to see. As my three friends has accepted, as do many. We accept things as they are, because of our sense of powerlessness to make a difference in the world, which seems pervasive in many of us. This fear we have, of not wanting to connect, could stem from this fact. Thus we remain, reluctant observers.

Wars will happen, eventually it will die off. And, it always goes away, fades into oblivion. Just as the innocents, who are but, 'collateral damage'.

We are torn between sense and reality. Which embeds in us, copious amounts of scepticism, confusion and distortion. Our senses, tells us, that what we are seeing, if we decide to take a peek, or to our worst fear, connect with the world. That, this is not real, we might think. We are all sincere, I am sure, when we express shock at the atrocities of man. Atrocities that we have bared witness to for millennia. The ancients speaks of war, not of atrocities or barbarity. For they spoke of a time not historically, but contemporarily. They speak about the glories of war, of great victories and conquer, which was inculcated into our 'short' history. And the stories we may tell, whether with pride or rancour. Important yes, but it blinds, and makes us feel that the details were 'not' important. How terribly brutal those wars must have been. Human beings killed, not by 'smart bombs', 'precision guided missiles', or 'drones'. Which targets 'very specific individuals', and is 'always accurate'.

But theirs were up close and personal, this ensured accuracy, as they had no sophisticated weaponry. Those 'others' were slain with axes, spears, swords, maces. Or, whatever comes to hand, sticks and stones even. Or, the horses and elephants the elites rode on to battle. It was man against man, man against woman, and man against child. Every battle field soaked in blood and gore. The savagery and indignity of rape, never to be known, were never told, as the victors are narrators of history. Who would admit then, even record such barbarism and atrocity. These modern adjectives were not known to them. But surely, there must have been that feeling of guilt and loss. In the midst of the battle they did not think and could not. But after surveying the battle field, must have wondered. What, was all this for? Is this piece of land worth the slaughter? They should have warned us that it is not worth it. Put it on paper, or chiselled it on stone, as *Asoka* did, they told us what happened. That was sufficient for their purposes, and must be sufficient for ours.

There is no possible way to strain the imagination. It may be possibly short circuited, due to some internal abnormality, or external stress. I cannot answer this question, regarding the absence of imagination. But I think logically, as well you. And, how far logic is taken depends on thought and imagination.

History is information, it is meant to be taken apart indiscriminatingly, and lessons extracted. Not taken apart and put back together as zealots do, every incarnation of them. They do not close their eyes to history, only to the parts that make them feel inferior, but do celebrate the parts that does not. We can learn a lesson or two from our zealot friends, I believe. My dear friends, the Doctor, the Shia and the Sunni, are not zealots. At least, I did not think so, but assume that this must be the case. For no one professes to be, but if you walk and quack like one, obviously. The lessons learned, from our observations of such individuals. Should caution us, to the dangers of relegating our inherent values, to the point of dismissal.

I am a 'good' man, I live in a decent and stable country. Educated, has never killed or been to war, and has never gone hungry. These facts I believe, and many others, which are not necessary to examine, being, but foregone conclusions. Nevertheless, what is important, is that my existence and place in this human ecosystem, was shaped by them. It made me the person I am.

Location, location, location, as the Americans say, seems to be what it is all about. But it's not that simple, if by the accident of birth, you were born in one of the many war ravaged countries. People in developed countries may never consider how lucky they are. Though some might, after seeing images of poor people on television, the few seconds of it.

What is striking to me, on visits to many so called 'advanced' countries? Is the lack of international content in their mainstream media, even persons I come in contact with, seems unaware of many current world events. It is almost, as if they are being shielded, as a child would, from seeing the bad things in the world. But those unfortunate children, born in poor countries, have no choice, their eyes are not shielded. For them, it is not about location, but, about existence, however terrible it is. There is no suburban utopia to move to with the parents, if they are unhappy with the noise and pollution, or the quality of 'private' schools in the city. There is no choice, about what they shall have for breakfast, cereal, bacon and eggs, I wonder?

No, for them, it is only if they eat today, or this week even.

Those who are kidnapped, to be taken away as child soldiers and sex slaves. Forced to kill and perform unspeakable acts for amusement and pleasure. Bearing scars, and obvious mental trauma, when interviewed years later. Still displays, that sense of human spirit. What do we expect of them? Caught in a never ending cycle of poverty and violence. That, they would attempt, such dismal display. Inevitably to be diminished!

It is all they have, the last drop of hope.
The 'feeling' to be human.

We all think about it, and ask ourselves. Why is there, so much suffering in the world? I am a very successful businessman. Why can't 'those' native brothers be more like me? I dragged myself out of poverty, and dismissively point out, that they can do the same.

We all have this sense, not of superiority, but difference. But how can we be different? We do not look that different? This might be puzzling to many, some probably, have never even questioned. What's the difference between the peoples of the North and South, West and East? Well, it would seem, that since race has been discredited as a theory. We should then distinguish ourselves, humans that is, by geography.

People of the South and East are now inferior. North and West superior. Since science has proven that we are all the same, and some brains, are not the size of walnuts, as the early racist's claims. As it is not about race anymore, surely it's about geography. And it so happens, they are correct, well, in a sense. But that geography determines development is subjective. The rise of China, as a major superpower, the staying power of Japan, and, the remarkable comeback of India, never mind its drawbacks, should now dispel that notion, just as the racial theory was. Why then the disparity, between these three countries, and what caused it? All three are ancient civilisations, why so different, in terms of development then. To answer this question, we must turn to history. More precisely, the history of colonisation.

Japan was never colonised, China to a limited extent, but India, fully. Interestingly, before the British arrived. India enjoyed almost one quarter of the world's trade. After they left, the country's world trade were down to a minor percentage. The Brits made India poor in exchange for democracy, these Indians should feel lucky they inherited the Westminster system. For they could not figure out a better way to govern, these ancient civilisations knows nothing.

We Europeans, have it all figured out, we are civilised, we know how to 'rule and get rich'.

I wondered sometimes, if the Europeans gathered together some centuries ago. And devised some sort of sinister back-room plot, designed, to take over the world. Or, it may have happened spontaneously. Now, we know, draw your own conclusion, the chicken and egg conundrum. However, we do know based on language, who were more successful. You are certainly correct, if anyone says the French and the British.

On every continent, the footprints of colonials are present. Their deeds laid bare for all who choose to see, as they raped and plundered every country. "Feeding of the blood of the colonised like parasites" as a professor once told me. All the problems, in all these countries, on every continent, are directly 'attributable' to the Europeans. This, there is no doubt about, for they planted the seeds of hate, and cultivated mistrust. So that they can reap, the sour fruits of primordialism. Where none existed, they were falsely created.

As they did in Rwanda, the Tutsis are elegant and civilised, fair in complexion, with straighter noses. And the Hutus not, in fact, they were built for hard work, Tutsis to govern. They have helped us run this wretched place for so long, now, we owe it to them, to be our successors. This had to be some sick and twisted plan, calculatingly, doomed for failure. May be it was just there way of doing things. They ruled as a minority for so long they must have thought, they can also do it.

The European's grand political strategy of 'divide and rule' is the legacy that would ensure that the formerly colonised, remains divided. Hoping to come back sometime in the future, for rents due from their successors, the ones they anointed. Of all, France in this regard is shamelessly the worst. For they have had a hand in everything that happened politically in francophone Africa, very long after the independence era, and the world knows about this. The British adopted this strategy in every country they ruled. In India, they took the latent varna system, and repurposed it, for their own political ends. Ensuring divisions, which no one must have previously occupied themselves about, even felt.

The Brits attempted to divide Africans and Indians in Trinidad. And for good measure, since the population were evenly split, further subdivided the Indians, between the Hindus and Muslims. Luckily for us, we occupied a fledging industrial state. With much abundance, good health and education. That after independence, the seeds of British division, did not take root, it could not.

As the conditions required for conflict, were not present.

This must have been our golden age. As we found our identity as one culture and one people, Regardless of race, or that 'thing' called religion.

An identity that would unite us.
As we have never been in any wars for independence.

Many great minds emerged from this post-independence era. And, most famous of course was Sir VS Naipaul. There are many others, lesser known. For they were not as proficient in the 'Queen's' English, as Naipaul was. Writing in our unique dialect, or singing as our calypsonians do. Were only able to reach the rest of the Caribbean, and diaspora too. It would seem that, we are constrained by our ethnic 'Caribbean' identity. Which we cater to in its small 'masses'.

When I think about it, seems that we are confined, not only by size, but in mind. One that has been 'inculcated' into us, forced fed. That sense that we are of 'small numbers'. That we come from 'small countries'. And, we do not have a place in the wider world. It irritates the hell out of me, when I hear these pseudo-intellectuals speak of 'small island developing states'. Connotations negatively loaded, as they relegate us, to under-developed stage. Hoping to get the crumbs off the developed nations' plates. This is a mind-set we must shake off. Or risk forever being trapped, in that 'small mindedness'. One that, they wish for us. It is like, we do not matter to the rest of the world. We do, they came looking for us, and still do.

Our history books tells of the Carib and Arawak. The poor indigenes of the Caribbean. And how they were conquered, suggested willingly, by the Spaniard. But how were they conquered? Not by converting them to Christianity. But by slaughter, imagination…remember. My son who is thirteen, does not like history. I tell him all the time, history is very important. His disillusionment, I realised only this week, was not about the subject, but of content.

Referring to the world's map, on my study's wall. He asked, Daddy, what about the Carib and Arawak. Not knowing much about them, except how they 'built' their huts, and what they had for breakfast. Which he has built a model of, by the way, apparently, very important for their curricular. I cannot imagine why this is important, hence his confusion. This is very upsetting, and more so, since he is not the only child. All children are looking for answers, and we are not giving it to them. Hungry for the knowledge that is not taught in his school, or any other for that matter. He asked in an open ended manner, and intelligently I must say. For it elicited from me a very lengthy discourse about the origins of these peoples. And, how they came to have occupied these shores.

Daddy, why don't they teach history like you? Ritchie, you cannot be taught history, you must learn history, you must feel it, and no teacher can give that to you. They can point out things to you, but you must use your imagination to make sense of it. I thought I was finished, Daddy, he persisted. As he sat on the recliner, waiting for my 'learned' answer. How do you know that the map is correct? I was initially shocked at the question, posited. After coming to terms with the depth of his inquisitiveness, mustered a response. "No, it is not, not all of them at least". "I don't think all the countries are the sizes as they put on the map", he said. "Yes, people lie, they never tell the whole truth". As I point to the legend at the bottom right hand corner of the map. "This is why, it is their proof, that what they are illustrating is correct, and we have to assume that it is correct", I said. "For it can verified or disproven".

Our Anglophile expat, hero to many, but not to all. Must have figured this out very early in his life. He saw the big picture, knew his place, and where he wanted to be. The fact that he apparently turned his back on Trinidad, and not of his hubris and arrogance. Is the reason why I think, Trinis do not consider him anymore, as one of us. We have recognised his achievements, and awarded to him our highest honour. But 'I' would have given it to him despite his great achievements. Just 'only' for the fact, that he knew what he wanted, and sacrificed everything, moved mountains, to get it. The fact that he came from an 'island nation' did not confine his imagination, to thinking small. He did not forget his origins, since he would often speak of how strange he felt in a foreign land. We are so 'unforgivingly' clingy, that we turn our backs, on those who have left our shores, 'as they attempt to find their place in the world'. Many have suffered from this cold shoulder syndrome. So much so, that it is difficult for them to pick up the pieces, so to speak, if or when, they do decide to return home.

The Nobel Laureate may not have been thinking about the bigger picture, that is, the subject we are discussing. But surely must have had the inclination. Concerned more about the self, than society and country, and, 'his' place in the world. Decided, that his mark 'must' be made. Which no one should disagree! He must have figured out the methodology, of linking his future with history. That if you want to know where you are going. You must know where you are. And, you only know where you are. If you know, where you came from.

As countless millions have done before. We must use our imagination in a logical way, in order to make sense of history. How else can we know, where we are, and where we are going? Should we throw up our hands in abandonment? Just because, we cannot figure out what is happening in the world. And how, we have come to reach this point. Is it the point of no return? No one can say, for we cannot predict the future. However, we can certainly 'soften' the realisation of our present state. If we knew, that what we are experiencing is not 'human's existence' natural order. Regardless of what we were led to believe. Our history was never one of total anarchy, leading to chaos. For even in anarchic societies, order we will inevitably achieve.

A body will remain in a constant state, unless compelled by an external force, to do otherwise. The Shia and Sunni of the Middle East, have coexisted for centuries. So has the various castes of India, and the Hutus and Tutsis. They have all recognised themselves, as belonging consanguineously, and contiguously by race. Despite particular beliefs and unbounded territories. There must have been quarrels, raids and tribal wars. But were usually settled, in some form or fashion. They did not consider themselves as different. And whatever differences they saw and felt, amongst themselves, was not serious enough, to warrant any protracted animosities. What changed all of this? Is what we must focus on? Even, if we have never pondered this question, we must do so now, for the time has come.

Adolescence we may think of, as only a period of our lives. A time of much uncertainty, as we try to figure out who we are. Am I a boy or a girl, I must be one or the other, for I cannot be both. Though I feel this way, how is this possible, it cannot be? We are confused, as biology presents us with hard evidence, the body. But the brain, the mind is saying something else. As we have determined adolescence, and confined to a particular period of time and development. We must recognise, the types of questions we asked of ourselves, then. Am I a boy? Yes, am I a girl? Yes. Am I both? No.

Understanding that you are different then, is not indifference. But 'not' accepting who you are, may lead to. As we may have provided ourselves with resounding answers, when faced with such questions. …

…In our 'for some' forlorn years.
For such, we have been thrusted upon.
Questions, of our present conditions.
Just as in our adolescent stage.
We are now being shook 'violently'.

Chapter One

And wonder, where we are

A re we there yet? As children always excitedly ask. No we're not, your trained eyes tell, that you have not seen any indication of your 'impending' destination. Not yet son, not wanting to express your own thoughts of frustration. You answer reassuringly, and somewhat optimistically, don't worry, we'll be there very soon. 'Several' hours later, the pink and purple signposts of Disney World comes into view. You don't have to say a word, it is there for all to see. But yet you say, 'we're here' as if he did not know this already.

I said this, I say this every time we visit. For each time to let my son know, that I have brought him to a 'magical' place. The scrupulous among us would see signs in the form of indications. Not being hard proof, but still able to ascertain from this limited source, for them compelling evidence. That they nearing, or, have reached their destination.

How do you know when reflecting on your country?
That you are near, or, you have reached a magical place?

No, no, no, magical places are only theme parks, where children can realise their dreams of unlimited happiness and freedom.

Or, that mental state of bliss, adults experience, under drugs and drinks. The few hours of, followed by 'fantastical dreams' that comes to an end by morning, hence escape.

Our conditions does not permit this sort of 'fantasy'. So get back to the real world, this plane. Since we cannot speak of such places and make references? How must we then view, our present circumstances? If we cannot compare, to where we should be at least. I will tell you in 'three' words, then close this book, for I will no longer speak:

'Deprivation', 'Frustration', and 'Aggression.'

I have just defined our entire existence. Hell, this does not explain anything, you say. It does not make sense to you, and never will. Unless we accept our reality, and that, we long for a better existence, anything but this one. So there, you have something to compare.

As we await, our untimely fate.
Like prey in the hunter's trap.
We have little choice but to ponder.
How on 'earth' did we get here?

Begins...

Next to a muddy four foot wide undulating track. There is a clearing, in this, the most densely populated slum near Kinshasa. Perched on a hillside just outside the main city, that is clearly visible, when the sky has not opened up to shower its 'blessings'. Sits *'Patrice'* on a semi mud covered red soft drink case. An eight year old rather small boy, with a mischievous look on his face.

No school today? No answer. Did not go to school, said the translator. I am so stupid, it's Wednesday morning of course, what was I thinking, now embarrassed. After pulling myself up for asking such a stupid question. I immediately placed myself in context. ...Why? Patrice is hungry, today he has not eaten any food, as Loraine goes on to translate. "Literally nothing", as she waves her hands palm down to demonstrate. "He's not just hungry, he's starving". A word never to be used anymore by me to describe my hunger for nourishment. I now say famished.

In all reality Loraine says, not anymore translating, but putting in her two cents, I guess. "Patrice will die of hunger or some related disease"…"maybe not today, but sooner or later he would join the hundreds of children, who die in this slum every year". Patrice does not live in the middle of the jungle in this vast country, he could smell the city from where he sits. He can with a short walk, visit the many food stalls just on the outskirts of the slum. But, he has no money, and no one to give to him. There is no definition for how poor this child is.

He is an orphan Loraine says, his mother died from cholera a couple of years ago. His neighbour looks after him. But, he still lives in the tiny shack he inherited from his departed

3

Mama. He does not know his father, his mother was raped in an IDP shelter, just before she arrived here.

Loraine is not a full time translator, she works for a small non-governmental Christian organisation, 'The Shepherd's Children'. You could literally cut her passion with a knife, which she oozed in every word she says. With interlaces of how Jesus loved the poor, and we should too, did not go down terribly, as atheists would think. Humanist values I thought, must transcend all aspects of life. If we can love somebody, just because they are poor, I do not know. But we can care, and should care, about the conditions they face in life…and if they survive.

How can we love 'that' we do not know, it is impossible, lacking connection. For Loraine having worked with these children for the past six years, not finding another after high school, have gotten to know them very well. Mama Nieve is unemployed, when she is able, would give a little food to Patrice, she has three children of her own, it is very hard for her, she really tries, but, ces't la vie. They are so poor, it is hard to understand the hopelessness, Loraine continues, "You would not see these things on TV, and if you did, you will never understand it".

Loraine's worst fear, is that Patrice might die of hunger, if he is not rescued very soon. He tells her sometimes, that he wants to work in the mines, where there's 'plenty' food. Most parents, almost all single mothers, are often duped by recruiters. Who promise that their children would be taken cared of. But the reality, these children are traded as would commodity. Are sold, and taken from mine to mine, abused physically and sexually, and, are forced to spend their days in the most squalled of conditions.

Being an orphan, Patrice is more or less on his own, he could disappear into the vast wilderness, with none the wiser. If he survives, might just end up joining one of the hundreds of armed groups that operates throughout The Congo, for the cycle continues. The very thing that makes us intelligent and loving creatures, is the very same thing that is shaping this poor child's life? It is the 'conditions' he has faced from birth. And, one that will continue to inevitably turn out, the man, which is the product of such a disaster.

It was not 'personal', no one targeted Patrice. And it is a fact, however unfortunate, we must tell ourselves, adopting a realist's view. For if we are to continue, as liberals do, would draw us into a sense of value. Realists understands the world better than us, and, must therefore put on that lens, which I do.

Patrice was not physically or mentally abused, from what unconscionable parents would do to a child. For he in fact felt love, shown by mother, Loraine and Mama Nieve. The potential violence he 'may' eventually exhibit. Would 'not' be the result of repressed hostilities. Lashing out at those who made him suffer needlessly, as we have witnessed in many developed countries. But, he would lash out against the 'system' that made him into 'this'. 'This' what he knows, not knowing what the 'other' Patrice would be? Enjoying good food and music, with great friends, kind and loving, and 'nonviolent'.

It is a puzzle to me, that many parents from Trinidad, would often spank their children for being rude, or acting out in a spoilt manner. But their children do not take a gun to them at the first opportunity. Knowing where they came from, and the sense of appreciation, that is sometimes instilled into them 'forcefully'. Would often…lead to them saying:

I'm glad…my mother straightened out my ass.

There will always be that feeling of indignation as Patrice tries, to make sense of his reality. Not finding alternatives, he would adapt to his surroundings. Pictures framed in his mind of atrocities committed by those around him. May change his mental state, but not to the 'detriment' of his personality, which was shaped by love and human attachment, so fleetingly he experienced as a child, but nevertheless ingrained.

He will suffer trauma and lose his sense of reality, but would not allow this, to reduce his sense of morality. And his aspirations for a better life, man's inherent desire. Conditions do not change human nature, for this is fixed, and based on needs. For that conditions change 'human behaviour' we must assume is real, as history demonstrate. This trap many has befallen, as conditions seems to dictate.

The conundrum of conditions.
Were we created by, or do we create?

Patrice's descension into the 'Abyss' started with the accident of birth, and, a life of poverty that eclipses any dreams he could unearth. This is a fact of life, as those born of such conditions, knows of nothing else. As we look at people and wonder why, for so long have been, in their present predicament. Poverty cripples its subjects with feelings of hopelessness, that it matters not what they do, they can never get out of this state.

6

It is our worst disease, and it determines every facet of our existence, in a downward spiral of despair. For even in some twist of irony, it is difficult to make light of this. I will however, in what would be my damnedest, since it is not my intention to get you depressed, but to shed light on this very important subject.

I drove past a gentleman many years ago, reasonably slow, for I had time to notice the expression on his face. I regret not having stopped, I do not know for what, but I am haunted by this thoughtless flop. Would I have just said hello, as some weirdo, or, offered him a lift, if he was not going in my direction, I would have had to go out of mine, what then would I do?

I remember him as if it was yesterday, but must have been, over fifteen years ago. He was a middle aged light skinned Indian man, average height with a full head of greying hair. Wearing an untucked white short sleeved shirt, he appeared dishevelled. But the expression on his face, is what struck me. For he had a look not of worry, but of 'daunted hopelessness misery'. Was his, a face of despair? Can one express this to such an extent, that it transcends them? I think of this sometimes, wondering whatever became of him. I will never know, but I do know one thing. I would never want to be in 'conditions' that I look like him.

Sad, I was myself guilty, of not wanting to connect.

Politicians have used poverty and our feelings of despair against us, ever since they were 'invented'. Almost certainly not kings, for they the richer their subjects. Politics therefore, would seem not conducive for a wealthy nation. Since it has been weaponised to create such conditions. As it is said and one would have to believe, religion started when the first smartman came upon a fool. So has this state of affairs been used as if a tool, for those to acquire and hold power, as the majority of any country has never been the rich, ergo, it serves their interest.

So briefly I will tell you in a paragraph or two. How I think we have reached these conditions, and hence, that not to do. We have not been able to resolve conflicts, because of our denial that the solutions lie in our hands, for if we do, our complicity would be revealed. Since conflicts now, it has turned out to be 'inevitably' man-made, so to the conditions.

It is a 'cycle' which must be revealed.
And, understand we must, for us to be healed.

Inherited Poverty, we did no doubt, for we walked bared feet on dirt, in mud. Lived in caves and trees like animals do. Thought we were like them, as we like them, would run around too. We left behind our four legged companions as our intelligence grew. Surely not all, for we kept a few. Our dog the best companion, we always knew. Would rival always our brethren few. As we did and expanded, our intelligence would now be 'corrupted'. We would grow and become one, enjoy the fruits of our hard labour, second only to none. As we thought, wealth was not created, but, extracted. There was only so much however, but, much more could be retracted.

What to do, as there was 'doubt'.
But surely, there was so much 'lying' about.

We inherited '*poverty*', and through a series of destructive practices, created further poverty. It is a cyclical process that is very difficult to escape in severely divided societies. The extreme cases, which are very obvious to everyone, are of former colonies.

The point here is 'laying blame', by recognising, that the 'despicable' act of colonisation, started the 'ball rolling'. Severely divided societies we can be sure, were 'created' by those who wished to 'exploit' our differences for gain…to sustain. Parasites would leave the body of its dead host in search of another, so did the many colonisers, as their countries could no longer. Conditions they had to 'falsely' create, in the countries they would come to inhabitate.

Differences we have never known, of our hair, height, nose and home. Would be used as markers to define…separate… divide us. Where there was no difference of 'obvious' physicality, they would then 'resort' to religiosity. To exploit what you own under the ground, in the trees, streams, or, 'whatever' flies around. They would collect samples and build museums, as a testament to you. Of the flora, fauna and figurines too. As Leopold and the others, would often do.

It was a patronising gesture, one would have to assume.
To assuage the guilt, in which, they must have been consumed.

A conference was held in the European Metropolis, to divide the spoils of the Basin, so less populous. What they did, there was no doubt. For they pitied him 'the poor', for by his lack of brain and brawn…would use this 'clout'.

They spoke of the 'heart of darkness' and one must 'wonder'. Did they mean, the depth of 'unknown mystery' and 'unfulfilled plunder'? Could not be the colour of the man's skin, as history has provided, they would also do…to their next of kin.

The 'King' newly crowned. Would christen thus, his private estate, 'The Free State' which he would proudly call. A contradiction in terms, if there was ever one. He never visited as most Kings would do their subjects, but ruled by decree, through his many 'objects'. From his palace so adorned with wealth and splendour. He would implement the harshest measure of 'forced labour'…'amputation' and 'murder'.

No subtle words can express the greed and desire that Leopold possessed. For what he created, was the first man-made disaster! That when he left, there were 'ten million dead'.

His departure from 'our' earth we would 'celebrate'
as Vachal Lindsay would epitate:

Listen to the yell of Leopold's ghost
Burning in hell for his hand – maimed host,
Hear how the demons chuckle and yell
Cutting his hands off, down to Hell.

But, the 'conditions' he fashioned, would have far reaching consequences very long after. For when he did abdicate, his sovereign would then create, not the state that was free…as he, but one that would ensure, there was 'never' any 'unity'. From the Kivus rich, in minerals like gold, they would set forth their quest, for ultimate control.

By force if they must, but if we use our 'proxies'.
We would conceal…our lust.

The Conflict

There are struggles taking place across The Democratic Republic of Congo. Which gives the semblance of a rudderless ship, upon the turbulent waters the ocean, adrift. However, what brings their particular state into sharp focus, and, contrasts so radically with other African countries, are the levels of violence displayed. Particularly in certain parts of the country. This very extreme forms of violence, are driven by resource competition. To give you an idea, despite past exploitation and the many years of corruption. The Congo still has an estimated mineral reserve, valued at over Twenty Five Trillion, in US dollars. That is correct, 25,000,000,000,000. The numbers, just to put things in perspective. It is all about greed, it has always been about greed.

From the King of Belgium, to the state of Belgium, to the state's politicians, to the many warlords, and now armed groups, operating throughout the mineral rich provinces. Communal strife, they have always known, but the tensions began during the colonial times and continues today. It has been the source of ethnic violence never to be unbroken. The Hutu and Tutsi are considered as foreigners and invaders by the many indigenous ethnic groups. But long before there were known borders, there have been migratory movements into the fertile Kivus. These communities therefore, considered themselves as indigenous, at least, as welcomed guests.

Conflicts began after the Belgians, in order to manipulate ethnic power dynamics. Promoted and encouraged mass immigration of Rwandans into the region. It is a requirement thus, to consider, as contemporary events does not exist in a vacuum. We must look at the conflict from a historical perspective, the history of the conflict, as it was caused by the conditions created by the short-sighted actions of the colonials. As memories of displacement and inequity would now influence the actions of politicians, regional leaders, chiefs and even the average citizen. Ethnically induced competition henceforth, would become one of the main drivers of conflict in the Kivus.

The Congo has experienced two major wars. Not the first, nor the second they fought with a foreign force, as in an invasion. For conditions on the ground were rife for influence and manipulation. So if you cannot succeed by ballot, then bullet. As 'implosion' now it seems, to be a sure-fire means of securing victory.

It is clear that the biggest threat to the state lies within. So it is important to focus on the survival of and conditions people live in. The fragility of the state, one must assume, was caused by decades of neglect, in which it was subsumed. As if a war of attrition, it fights with itself, in a never ending cycle of poverty, destruction and death. Millions go hungry every day, the displacement camps, where the poor seek shelter, are often washed away. The savagery of deep and dark violence are meted out, on those who would show…reluctance.

Conflict and violence are just one aspect of the ills facing The Congo. Exploitation, greed, and corruption are the others. As conflicts are but a manifestation of deeper problems. Exploitation, greed and corruption are the 'source' for others.

It is not the result of, but the source of some of the worst issues facing the Congo. Worst of all is child slavery, with an estimated amount of children, numbering in the thousands. Working in very dangerous conditions, some, as soon as they can walk, as they tag along with their parents.

Coltan is the new game in town, and much easier to mine than other artisanal minerals. Children can earn a dollar or two if they are lucky, most times to take back to their families, or to buy food for themselves.

It is a heart breaking, cold and cruel existence.
It is a living hell filled with hopelessness, pain, and
suffering.

Patrice, at such a tender age, will face the tough choice whether he would emigrate, to one of the many mining provinces so far away. Should he leave behind what he knows for a life uncertain, no one can tell. The people that care would surely discourage, as they know best. For he does not know what awaits him. There are rumours of the horrors children face, of lives lost, and the dreams that fade.

But anything would be better he thinks,
what's the worst that can happen.

Chapter Two
Into the Abyss

In 'this' place where Patrice would sit, pondering questions he could not fathom, for his young mind not too equipped. Which, for some reason, always bring him back to where he 'should' be, that place where he could be happy and free. Free from this life, so hard, he was brought into, not blaming Mama, for she was in this too. If I could only get a job, he thinks, I could eat every day, I would help my little brother, my new family. I would go to school and take him with me, for he too would like to live, why shouldn't he?

He remembers the bicycle they once saw, down at the edge of the slums, where he and Marcel would often go, to see what it is like on the 'great beyond'. It was so shiny it sparkled, it must have been so clean, and this is why it looks like this. Everything 'outside' this place is so clean. Marcel does not know these things, so I had to tell him, I have to tell him everything, that…

> *…I can ride that bike better than she.*
> *Fly higher and faster than could…anyone see.*

Marcel is an orphan too, very unfortunate, for he neither knew his parents…two. Unlike Patrice who had but a 'glimpse' of what it is like to have such a privilege? Unable to grasp its importance, Marcel will grow up living a life of wonder, for some irrelevance. For he was abandoned outside the slums five years ago, when he was just a 'tiny' two. Many have looked after him, he would seek help where he could find, and often do. They would provide shelter under their rickety wood and tarpaulin roof, where he could see the rain pour, from the many holes in the wooden crates walls and door. There was so much 'warmth' as Marcel would remember. The home sweet home, for anything beats the weather.

He now stays with Patrice in the tiny shack they share. He considers him his 'big brother' for there is not...another. So often, thinks he has betrayed, when he is given some food by the many families he once stayed...took shelter. Patrice shares more than his shack. For he has instilled in his little brother... the one he never had.

> *The sense of hope…for them daring.*
> *That one day we will be of…and flying.*

Patrice would sometime later, be introduced to such a character. One who would bring hope of anew, of something different? That would now change his worldview. For him, this has been his 'dreaming' for one day to come he would be...teeming. Ready to take on the world...he knew could conquer. The time has come, I cannot hesitate. If I don't decide now, it may be too...late.

A rather shady man, Leo was he, Patrice could not put finger on, but, does it matter now? Patrice has been looking forward to this day, for as long as he can remember. A chance to leave this slum, a chance for a life...better. Leo would wear his dark glasses even in the shade, and Patrice would think this is why it was made. Made to see things clearer when it was dark, so should he get one too, for times when it was hard?

To make out the 'people' good and 'bad'.

Patrice was 'elated…' with promises of education and food in return for household chores, anybody could do this. Looks like a better way to succeed, than a 'life' in the mines, who knows where 'that' may lead?

The chance to get an education, and a family too. This is so unreal, I can't believe my dreams are coming through. Mama Nieve and Loraine would be so happy, that I would succeed. Surely they would not try to stop me, if they do, then I would just…leave. I have no choice, I know what's best for me. I would take Marcel and we would join a family. We will have food every day and a chance to play. But I will never forget Mama Nieve and what she has done for me. All the love and kindness she has shown, since I was a baby. I 'swear' on my mother that I will return, to take Mama and the children away from their little home. When I do…I will be their hero. I will wear the superman shirt you see all the time, its blue I think with a big sign.

Heroes help people, that's what I will do, and, I will shine.

Leo is well known child trafficker, almost impossible to find, since the police has been looking for him, for quite some time. He has this way of blending in with people, as a chameleon would in the jungle. He would dress, walk and talk and is fluent in many dialects. He is known in the underworld as the 'Shady Leo', he runs a lucrative business with a coltan mining operator, based in Lubumbashi. He supplies labour for the mines his former army buddy operates, so the story goes, at least. The real prize for them is children, who are rarely paid, and when they do, are often short changed, out of the few dollars they would have made. They cannot fight back, they are small and weak, and 'so' desperate.

The mines are many days away, Leo often use modest forms of transport, sometimes enclosed trucks, to get them to their destination, that desired spot. The mine's surroundings are littered with makeshift plastic and tarpaulin tents, there is no running water, sanitation and electricity…well forget. There is no supply of safe drinking water to be found, children drink from pools and what streams between their feet, it is heavily contaminated by the mineral's waste, adds a metallic flavour to the taste. By the few survivors they have been told, it is a wasteland, no eyes should behold.

Corporal Banza, or 'Cap' as he likes to be called, short for captain, which he never was. Cap operates a medium sized mining operation, in a very remote part of Lubumbashi. It takes hours to get there from the main town. You always happen to get there in the night, it does not matter what time you leave town, even at dawn. His operation is only but the first link in what is quintessentially, modern slavery. Cap sells the coltan to the middle men, who would then sell to the exporters. Cap could never sell directly to them, they purchase only from sanctioned middle men. It is not a complex process in the least, it is very simple. However, set in such a way that it creates, plausible deniability, if or when, 'never' it is exposed.

One of the extracted elements from coltan are used to make capacitors for mobile phones, computers, electric cars and many other electronic devices. Many huge tech companies stand accused of being complicit in child slavery that is happening in the Congo. The DRC is not the only source of coltan in the world, while they may have the largest reserve. Their methods of mining still remains very primitive, hence inefficiency. So their overall output percentage, maybe smaller than those of other countries, let us say Canada or Australia. But, what makes coltan more attractive from the Congo than other countries? Should one hazard a guess, that it is price, and about the process, of extraction using 'child' labour.

This is a true story, it was funny, but sad at the same time, I did not hold what the young lady said against her, maybe she did not know, at the time. May be it just never occurred to her that while chocolate do come from Belgium, but they just put together. "Belgian Chocolate…the best in the world" she said, had me 'confused'. At a Purdy's outlet, Ontario, some years ago, I happened to stop at mid-sized kiosk, situated in an opening to a corridor. Why I did, I do not know, for I am not a lover of chocolate, at least, that which is produced commercially. I would indulge however, in our local hand crafted chocolate bars, which is organic, and never too sweet.

Surely, that chocolate was only refined in Belgium. And, I am being too hard on her, for this is what she meant, or trying to convey. What would dispel this notion however, was the look on her face, when I said. "You mean Africa don't you. Or, Gran Couva chocolate, the best in the world". Much to her horror, gasped, wanting to utter the word 'impossible'. But did not, maybe she didn't believe me, she seemed perplexed. I did a simple search on its website, and found that Purdy's manufactures its own chocolate, which is sourced from the Ivory Coast, Ghana, Ecuador and Peru, some of the larger producers of cocoa in the world.

Trinidad's Trinitario, and others from the Americas, are those which are prized for their taste, and used as flavouring cocoa in chocolate production. Why would this cheerful las claim, that Belgium had the best chocolate in the world? I am still confused as to why she would say that. It was just that they have figured out the recipe for a fine tasting product, using beans and sugar taken from elsewhere, for which is given no credit.

Why would they then…for it has been like this for centuries. To neglect or deliberately conceal of the sources of materials, used in the in the production of processed foods like chocolate. Is an attempt one must conclude, to hide their complicity in the abhorrent practice of slavery, now child labour, which is often used.

This is an affront to human dignity and human rights? The conditions that creates the cycle of poverty drives the supply of cheap labour. Which is readily absorbed within these industries, at the very first stage of the process. It is detestable, and we must reject it.

But we choose instead, to close our eyes to the fact that millions of children work in these industries. Which is nice way of putting it, in slave like conditions, most often under very dangerous circumstances. For them it is a matter of survival, if they and their families eat. Bluntly, big corporations are profiting from the 'slavery' of children, and that is the bottom line. …Well maybe not, profit is.

"The essence of all slavery consists in taking product of another's labour by force. It is immaterial whether this force is founded upon ownership of the slave or ownership of the money that he must get to live".

— Leo Tolstoy

Slave Child

Who knew that 'I' would have been led?
To a life of prison.
Just because, how 'I' was bred?

Born and raised as my mother and father did.
To a life of bondage and slavery, we all agree?

'We' suffer our fate, at the 'hands' of the master.
Yelled upon, for all the breath, he could muster.

It is a terrible life, I wish for no other.
But just one day, someday, would find another.

I dream of play, when I work.
Even when 'all of my body' hurts.

I play 'all' the time, for 'I' am in, my 'mind'.
For even my thoughts, he wants to take away.
For each time, would shout.
Get back to work, stop dreaming 'about' you know better.

At nights, I listen to the mosquito sing.
For she brings me peace, before I go to sleep.

As a mother would, for her child so dear.
Sing me a lullaby, and make my 'pain' disappear.

In my shack, so damp and humid,
Deep inside the valley, of trees and bushes.

I hear a rustle, from a low waft of breeze.
Like music to the sound.
As the cricks, toads.
They move, around.

The dark of the night, brings me 'so' much happiness.
I can dream for hours 'until' the rumble of by tummy, awakes.

Of not hunger, but to see 'his' face.
The sickness I feel, cannot describe,
It's of pain and worry, no face can hide.

For this is dawn.
And 'thus' begins the new day.
Of pained, exists.
And 'dusk' can.
Not return, fastly.
For me, to escape.
The clutches of his gaze.
… So ghastly.

...Patrice awakes from what would seem an eternity, the thirty six hour drive from the slum to Lubumbashi. Still clutching in his hands, a dirty looking white plastic bag with some scraps of dried bread, which he wanted eat, but left for breakfast instead. His stomach wringing in pain from hunger and nausea, still managed to look to his side for his little brother. Fast asleep as he always is, only to awake with a slight shove, and the words 'get up'.

There were other children in the back of this 'enclosed' truck, a few only visible from the sharp rays on sun, piercing through the louvre type window. He spots the girl he talked to the night before, on one of the stops where they would go? Usually in secluded and bushy areas, out of the sight of strangers. Get out quickly, hurry, hurry, Leo would shout, for only ten minutes they had, they would scramble about. In the dark, then back on the truck, once again the hazardous journey begins.

Patrice did not ask her name, he is afraid of them, and freezes when he comes in contact with girls. Said, she was from same place. It was very late in the night when they were loaded up unto the truck, on a dirt road that lies between two sides of huge piles of rubbish, leading out of the slum. The place was very dark, and only under moonlight, might catch the faint glimpse of silhouettes lurking, and sounds of bottles clanking. Pray not to be caught here alone in the night, they do terrible things to little girls, she was often told.

She told Patrice that out of the twelve of them, that she is the luckiest, that she is going to work with a very rich family. Immediately his mind zoned off, since he did not count, he tended to believe the former part of her account, but the latter did not. He was also told that both he and Marcel are going to stay with a very rich family. How many rich people are there? He questioned himself, afraid to ask the 'girl'. We will see who gets to stay with the richer family, in his mind, that question will never survive.

Looking at her, while she slept, not far from him that final morning. Could help himself but think, look at that 'liar', then she opened her eyes and looked directly at him. I caught you, he felt sort of embarrassed, but melted. This is his first experience, seeing a girl this way. Except of course Mama Nieve's daughter Minerva, a six year old and the third of her children. 'But she is like a sister to me, she can't like me like this girl. I wonder if all the girls at my school would like me…as she'.

The double door of the truck swings open, a surge of breeze and blinding light hits his face and eyes, within a minute the sweat on his body dries. We are here, he shouted, what sounded like Leo. He grabbed Marcel's hand as they made his way to the back of the truck. In the two minutes or so, his eyes became almost adjust. Leo was standing there with a 'strange' smile on his face. 'He looked as if he was happy, I will not disappoint him, he'll see'. Making his way down from the truck, all he could see was nothingness, all around them. Maybe we just stopped again…to pee, he thought. Get down from the truck, everybody, follow me…as they did.

Child 'Slave' Labour, is the worst form of domination one could have over another. As if you do not matter, and to you should no one, not brother, sister, father, or mother. The master has total control over you, the sooner you realise, the better for you. Your little mind 'need' put at ease, knowing the master only, you must please. The power lies in his hands, now it is taken from yours. That growing sense of less-ness, will not soon erode, it will become greater as the days, months, and years go by, leading you to wonder...why? Why I feel no connection to the world anymore? He would raise his fist and threaten me, use his stick to poke me. Finish your work you worthless dog, rip my ear until it bleeds, he does this with all his might, his face reveals.

For if I was a dog, I would surely bite.

The harrowing accounts of those held in slavery and servitude, all speak of the 'violence' meted out to them, apparently for no good reason, other than bringing them into total submission. The ignorance of not knowing what is about to happen is common in all cases. Only in hindsight, would one realise what had happened, how they became trapped.

This is the case for millions of adults who are held in slavery all over the world. Fortunately, they are adults, and can fight back, if they have the courage and will to do so. What about the children who are unable to, how can they fight back or escape from the clutches of slavery? The world it would seem is not designed for the meek...the weak. Who would they turn to? As would your son or daughter to you.

Put yourself in their shoe, if this is the only world you knew? You are in a world, where no one care. If you live or die, and the lost dreams, you once held dear.

The world and I, like an ever growing ocean.
Separates my 'reality' from my 'illusion'.

'Don't think about it, just do it, this is your life.' This is not my life you think. Since when did this become my life?

No, I want to be a teacher. I just want to save enough money so I can go to school. People like you don't go to school. Listen, this is your work, as he grabs you by the arm, forget that crap. Smacks you in the head, you were born for this. 'What did your parents do, were they rich? They worked right here'. Well, now they are dead, what did that get them? I wish I was dead, I am nothing. I watched some children go to school once, they looked so happy. I wonder what that feels like, to wake up, your parents are there for you. Mother makes you breakfast... give you something to eat, bread...tea.

I feel like I have sold my soul to the devil, just so I can eat, can I live on fruits like the animals do, they look happy, I would be too. Does everyone do this, give away the freedom, so they would not die of hunger? If only my mother was here, I cry every night, and day, hoping one day I would see her face, she would tell me, don't worry my baby, everything will be okay. When I get big, I will show him, I will rub it in his face when I buy this place. I will hit him on the head, and slap his face, I will push him to the ground, and tell him he is worthless. Just as he did to me for all these years, I am filled with such misery, I cannot bear the thought of myself, he is right, I am worthless. I am made to feel that he is right every time he hits me, why doesn't he like me? I work hard, the others are bigger and can do much more. I do not understand, why he does not know this. No longer is it important to me, as my dreams are fading away. It is like the disappearing land, as I drift slowly into the deepest parts of the sea.

So this is it, this is my life.

As if he is god, or my father, or my mother, for he is none of these, but must still obey his every wish. He has power over me, 'he could push me to the ground and tell me to lie there, and I will have to'. How on earth can such behaviour be tolerated, I ask?

The constant verbal abuse and physical violence on 'slaves' are visited upon daily. Such behaviour, finds its source and is legitimised by the conditions created by society. More specifically, the culture in which violence is permissible. It has become the necessary means, the masters would use to subdue, overwhelm and maintain their 'stranglehold' on their victims.

There are societies that are not overwhelmingly violent. But there are many countries that are inordinately and absolutely violent, hence, the culture of violence. It is not uncommon to hear of stories of those who were, or are being held against their will. Usually in domestic settings, and even densely populated areas. It is not as they are being held captive in some remote plantation, in almost every instance, threats and violence is the main weapon used for compliance.

It is like hell, not quite, but almost there.

As if you are a walking dead, everything from inside is stripped away. There is no emotion, your senses are numb, as if disappeared. You no longer feel the pain from the blows you get. Hurry, hurry, you pray, take me now, do not delay. If you don't, I sure will, I will jump off this place, and soar till I reach my place, if death…it is?

You have tested, but still you refuse me. I have tried so many times to end this life, this life in hell, so full of misery. You have blessed so many, why not me? I have been dead since the day I was born. Give me death or give me slavery, surely I will take…mortality.

27

How can one be dead, and alive at the same time? I cannot be the only one, I have looked for faces, but see no sign, of anybody's, that looks like mine…of misery. You should be grateful, they say, by now you would have been dead. That life would have chewed you up, and spit you out, and they are right.

The same conditions that would have killed you.
Have brought you into slavery.

…Patrice and his friends follow Leo for several minutes through the dirt track, until they reach a clearing. Cap walks over, you will stay with my friend Cap for a few days. I have to make the arrangements for you to meet your families. The smiling Cap greets Leo, with a shoulder hug. Lovely, I thought there was more. They will do, this one looks strong, pointing at me, felt good, as I looked at the others, if I knew that this meant things to come, I would have thrown myself to the ground…feigned weak. You will like it here my friends, I will pay you five dollars when you work. Cap is a strange looking man Patrice thought. He had dirty clothes but wore a gold watch. A quite dark man, had very white teeth, which apparently he wanted all of us to see. There is plenty food…all around, says Cap. Looking around, all that Patrice could see was patches of bush…not even trees.

Chapter Three
War and Hunger

Patrice and Marcel would bond with Dalia over the months, as they found that it was better for them to stick together. Also, having Dalia around helped a great deal, Patrice found. Her enormous talent for conversation and quick wit, helped the three in securing food from the many adults who work in the mine. Usually consisting of tubers and green bananas, Cap would purchase from a gardener close-by. He shares them among the workers, but always deducts the money from their pay. Most of the meals they prepare in old dented aluminium pots, blackened from the plastic used as fuel to keep ablaze an open fire of leaves, grass and twigs. Fire wood is scarce, and must search for hours to get some. Which if they are lucky, would come across trees that were fell in clearing the way for mine operations. As the mines were not big, neither were the trees. It did not matter, it was worth the effort, having warn food was a comfort in this unforgiving place.

As the Second Congo War rages to the East, there was no indication whatsoever, in the little world of theirs. They would hear Cap speak of it, the few times Leo stopped by. The times he did, would also bring with him some people, who always stayed back. Once, an entire family, a father, mother and a little child, she could be about three. Cap has a few of them sorting rocks from the black iron they dig out of the ground, he says our fingers are nice and small for the job. The bigger children and the couple that came with us, does the digging and the filling of bags, eventually Cap told me, I would move on to this.

He told us that we would make enough money for the time that we are here, it is difficult to tell for how long they have been in there. As per Patrice's estimation, he thinks it is more than a year. As they await Leo's return with the good news their family has been found. So they are very disappointed, when he shows up, only to leave without saying anything. Hope lingers, but their fate, they would now have to resign to this place.

Cap is not too bad, he shouts at us all the time, to get the work done, but never hits us. He is well organised and strict, he gets this from the army that he served in for many years. Although dirty from the black iron dust, he always maintains a dignified appearance. His shirt always tucked, and his pants too, in his dirty 'worn' army boot. You could see signs that he is a good man, from the way he treats us. There are rumours that his entire family was killed by the leader of an armed group some years ago.

Joseph served in the army with Cap and Leo. Cap and Joseph were like brothers, they joined the army, though some time apart, were inseparable throughout the years. They shared everything, long before Leo made his way in. An annoying fellow who would talk for hours, and makes up stories as he goes along, he would string. He lies a lot, but remarkably they found out, Leo had a natural gift for getting things done, otherwise, getting results. He is very talented in the way he would use his connections, through his vast family networks, also never ending as the way he talks.

Both Cap and Joseph made plans for the future, they decided they should both early retire. Having been nearly killed, several times during the First War. Their plans from the beginning were to go into mining. But, they had different ideas on how to this should be done. Cap wanted the more conventional approach of prospecting. But, they would use their skills as former squad leaders, and would raise a small 'army' of sorts. They would pay them fairly, unlike what they were given in the army.

Joseph however, had very different ideas, a warlike and aggressive individual, wanted to organise along lines, as he did in the military. Their disagreements would not be realised, until sometime after they went into business. Leo could not imagine life in the army without the two men he looked up to the most. So much so, that he deserted and followed his leaders into the unknown, upon their retirement. Both men were very ambitious, knowing that they would have made excellent officers, because of their natural ability to lead men, and their 'industrious' minds.

Hunger

Marcel now eight, is happy all the time, at all times. The only thing that gets him worried is when he is hungry. And never for long as everyone likes him, so he gets food wherever he goes. He has been doing this since he was two, it is, as if he needs no one else. Not even his big brother, or Dalia, when it comes to finding food. He would even eat the roasted locusts, the local bush people would often give to him. It is tasteless, but crunchy, and the legs stick in his teeth. It is good protein though, he pretends he is eating chicken drumsticks, he would pluck out leg by leg, and crunch them down. Marcel is a growing child, and needs to eat. The human attachment he has with Patrice, and now Dalia, matters not one bit, when it comes to his stomach's emptiness. Growing up as he did, answers to the call of only this master, and must serve him when he calls. So out the door you go, feelings of bonds, for the pains of hunger is stronger than foolish love.

We say we are starving, but are we? Nourishment for us is in our kitchen's refrigerator, or right around the corner deli. Marcel's pain similarly is not of starvation. He is hungry all the time, because he fills up all the time on carbohydrate packed foods, which is gone in a flash. And it is this, that which gives him that lethargic feeling. Many adults who work in the mine are called lazy, if they doze off after eating boiled starchy foods. Luckily for Marcel, however under-nourished, he is alive. He is still better off than most children in other countries, suffering from mal-nutrition and starvation. For them it is a quiet and slowly creeping form of hunger. That brings about weakness and disease, eventually death. Never to tell the tale, of what a horrible companion hunger is.

Finding food is a full-time pre-occupation, not to mention health and education. The children who work in the mines are for some reason fixated on thoughts of going to school. Knowing, that it would be their one time chance to leave the misery of the mines. How easy for us, that we take for granted all the positive elements of our conditions, which has shaped our existence. Without giving a second thought of how lucky we are. Children like Patrice, Marcel, Dalia and the countless others, the millions who face so much obstacles at every stage of their development, or lack thereof. It is unbelievable, that they survive at all.

Patrice is getting bigger and stronger, which he credits to Cap. Who would often tell him: 'my boy, I will make you into a 'big' man, and no one will do you wrong'. He tells him that he should eat only green plantains and bananas, 'you ever see the silver back gorillas, they can rip a man in two…this is all they eat'. Cap spent many months in the jungle while he was in the army, half starved, they would partake in whatever was available. Patrice has seen the results, but is getting sick of the bland taste of the boiled fruits. The fruits have not matured enough to produce the sugars that gives that sweet taste. In any case, eating the soft mushy fruit is not conducive, for their type of hard work.

If Patrice had internet, unheard of at that time in most parts of Africa. He would have found out why it was so good for him, as Cap keeps suggesting: "One cup of boiled green bananas has over five hundred milligrams of potassium, and is a rich source of protein and vitamins. It is high in fibre and starch resistant, so it regulates blood sugar levels and manages weight, and health".

Again the problem with access to information. If he could just figure out a way to make this thing taste better, he often thinks. If he could find one of the many recipes for preparing green bananas into a delicious dish. Fondly called 'green fig' in Trinidad, Trinis have come up with a veritable handbook for preparing green bananas. If only Patrice had this information, access to information is a major setback and impedes the development process. The things Patrice could have done. The mouth-watering sumptuous delights he could have made, if he only knew how.

Finding great recipes from Trinidad, or from any other country for that matter, is only the tip of the iceberg. Information that could drastically change their lives, like the dangers of handling coltan and drinking the water that runs of it, could have been available. Information about the war that is taking place in their own country, and of the magnitude of the problems they are likely to face as they grow older, would lead them to prepare better for this challenging future. As they are unaware, everything comes as a surprise, the slightest challenge to their planned course of action is likely to have trajectory changing outcomes. Like ending up in the mines, and not finding a family to live with, if they had information they would have known how unlikely this was. As any computer savvy eight year old would be able to figure out.

War

War is the continuation of politics by other means, so goes the General's belief. But how does this accurately describe what taking in the Congo, or any civil war for that matter. According to him, we must look at war as a whole, and its constituent parts determined. The General was concerned not of wars fought amongst peoples, but of wars among nations. For much too long we have tended to answer such questions relating to civil wars with the same queries. 'Not' pertaining to belligerency among its people, but with those among peoples of different nations. For much of our existence we have asked ourselves such questions, why nations fight? That we lose sight, of the real conflict that is taking place, right under our noses. Millions of lives have been lost over the decades. Yet, we are consumed with thoughts of nuclear holocaust, and armed invasions. But, are not so much about those killed with small arms, and light weapons.

The Congo has never been a fully functioning democracy. Its turbulent history not only suggest, but proscribes in a sense, any form of normality. In the absence of efforts to alter conditions on the ground, that may be conducive for the safety, security, and development of its people. The country already weakened from decades of conflict, runs the risk of total collapse, leading to failed state. Conditions that have been created over the years. Has led to the capture of the state resources, by forces that runs counter to state legitimacy and supremacy. Usurping what would otherwise be the ultimate state authority, in the use of force and security.

In certain regions where vacuums are created, as no go areas for state forces, where the conditions are right to seize territory and resources. And the taxation of the local population, through violence, intimidation, and criminalization. Recognising that this state of affairs exist, does not mean accepting it, however, most deny its existence, hoping that one day, the problem would go away.

As states would, under different forms leadership, seek from other states, alignment and patronage. This is not the case however, for 'shadow' non-state actors, or even, de-facto state leaders, not recognised, or deny that they are, by states. As such, illegitimate non-entities may turn to middlemen, who then resort to multi-nationals for global access. To suggest that the wars of the Congo is the continuation of politics by other means, is to shut our eyes to the real problems that exists. One that the international community knows about, but nothing can be done about this, since it means challenging the very same system 'capitalist' as they are part of it. They deny that they are part of the problem, analogous to the demand for illicit drugs in the US that drives 'criminalised' conflict in Mexico.

It is rather convenient, therefore, to blame those who are 'under-developed' and prone to conflict and violence, for they know not better. They lack the means to see things clearly, because of their short-sighted greed, that, they would risk reducing to a wasteland, their own country, just to get rich.

...Upon their retirement from the army, Cap and Joseph with Leo in tow, already stationed in the Kivus, headed to the further north eastern area, bordering Uganda. Joseph had links to a Ugandan Colonel, he says, but Cap doubts, he would take the coltan off their hands? Cap thought that the Kivus was much too dangerous, that they would come into conflict with the armed groups that operate throughout the area. With much of their members infiltrated from the eastern countries, they hold no qualms in dispensing, whomever they come in contact with. They have nothing to lose, and can vanish across the border after creating chaos, in other words.

Cap settled his wife and two young children in Loda village, about fifty miles north of Bunia, the Capital of Ituri. Cap's and Joseph's retirement as it is called, really means the expiration of their contract they signed with the army. In most regions and armies around the world, contracts usually runs for about three years. It was late 1997, having had enough violence without profit, Cap and Joseph, and most of their batch, opted not to sign new contracts. The short intervening period following the end of hostilities between the rebels loyal to Kabila and government forces. Provided just the right opportunity to begin their venture.

Leo barely served out his first contract, followed, along

with six others of various ages and ranks. They would need much more man power to get the mine going, it was a good start however. Cap wanted a little distance from Joseph, whom he thought was a bit overwhelming. He suggested that they split up, taking each with them some of the men. They would stand a better chance, and cover a wider area. They did, after much hesitation from Joseph, along with three of the men managed to get some locals to help, only to be paid if they found minerals. Leo stuck with Cap, and with the three remaining men, managed as Joseph did, from some locals, secure help. Most of the men were married, with the exception of Joseph, and of course, Leo. They all saw this as an opportunity to make money finally, the married men especially. Most of their former superiors were involved in one way or the other, in some sort of 'illegal' activity that brought in some money.

Joseph enlisted when he was just seventeen, and served five contracts, Cap eighteen and served four. Not much age disparity between the two, Cap often wondered why they thought so differently. It could be their upbringing or the tribes they belonged to, Joseph seemed to have this chip on his shoulder, he is angry all the time, and with everyone. He speaks with a brutish tone of voice, often hate filled when really upset, he always wants to kill someone, even for the slightest transgression, sometimes totally out of context and for the smallest thing. No wonder he is not married, Cap would think. He feels sorry for his friend, and hopes that one day he would find some peace with himself.

The rainy season helped to some extent, loosening up the dirt and rocks in the two mines they established. Only a couple of miles apart, the terrain was very different. Cap had selected an area with many trees and over growth. Joseph, an area that was much clearer, he thought would be easier to work. Unfortunately for him the deluge of the November rains proved very difficult as it would flood most of the plain. It was very hard, and frustrating to say the least, for Joseph especially. Who had invested much time and money into his area of choice? Maybe they started at the wrong time of the year, but it always rains, they thought.

This simple act of diverging choices, reflects both of the men's character, and attitude towards achieving their goals. It will also signal the beginning of tensions, felt very early by Joseph, but, not by Cap, thinking both to be on equal footing and unanimous with their growth. Cap's initial and growing success, in now what appears to be 'his' mine, made Joseph feel somehow side-lined. Joseph's meagre returns, Cap would think, was because of the choices he made, not only regarding the mining area, he had chosen, but the many others, somewhat irrational choices he has made. Like passing up the opportunity to make officer, which obviously he felt not good enough for.

He's not in it for the long haul, Cap thinks. He wants to get everything right away, it's all about him, and no one else. He has no consideration for the people around him, his comrades, or, the poor peasants he convinced to work for him. Joseph's irreconcilable greed, with his lack of, what he thinks is ambition, puzzles Cap.

Chapter Four
Why we Fight?

I have a friend whom I must admit, admire greatly. And wonder why because, he is a 'kind of an ass' as people would describe others, as him...me? What makes us tick, as if we were in sync? Or, mesh as people would in thought, for we have nothing in common, but our dislike for others! What ties us, and, brings us in unity, is 'not' always I have realised... commonality. As people would think, because they have in common things...will automatically.

We all love the same things, that's true you might say. The birds, the infinite night sky, and the trillions of stars. The ocean so deep and blue, you can never deplete...matters not what you do. We can share the things we cannot 'have', 'hold' or 'take'. For those we can, surely, make no mistake. As sure as the sunrise, the time we all love...

...there will be a conflict...we must undertake.

We cannot own the ocean, but what leads to. The beach front property, or that swathe of land, that gives access to, that for which...we cannot 'without' do. It is what brothers and sisters fight over. What, countries go to war for. It is what Pakistan did to Balochistan after separation. Or what Russia did to Ukraine, in their quest for accession, and have succeeded, by the Crimean annexation.

The quest to take, to have, and to hold, the resources you conquer, seems two-fold. To have over another and to better those, it does not matter, whosoever. To gain 'supremacy' and 'suffer' them…the other. Land is but one resource, but the bounty that awaits, of resources soon we will discover. Adds thus, greater dimensions for greed, and the lust for power.

For those, will sow the seeds of unrest and chaos, violence and intimidation, and, outright war if they must. For nothing can hide your true motives, than noise. There is none other than conflict and death, to conceal one's real intentions. It is the ultimate 'deception', a gruesome 'masquerade'. Not of 'pomp' as in a ball, or the battlefield in which armies are arrayed. But a new portrayal.

'Maskirovka' as in Russian thought.
'Duplicitous' in the warlord's brain.

We do not fight over the ocean, but what is in it. The fish, and the minerals contained under…neath. For this is finite, not the salt, or the water you cannot drink. Their true motives are hidden, as arctic explorations are undertaken, just but an example. It is plain for all to see, except for those, who do so foolishly.

Some things just cannot be concealed, by their actions they would be revealed, their greed exposed for the world to see. The conditions they create, in one form or another. It is ethnic, as the warlord would say, we hate the other, annihilate them we must…

…chance they cannot … for them we are slaughter.

We compete for resources that are, but limited. The heat of the sun, or the wind that blows…not. It is precious we say, but not the lives lost, when we take it away. They can make more, we too, for that matter. It is a sacrifice, the greatest we must make, to get the upper hand, for what is ours we must take…

…at any cost, if we must.
We will slaughter all that comes across.

…There was no expressed animosity towards Cap. As the 'imagined' conflict raged in Joseph's head. Cap had no idea, not a clue. He would be taken totally by surprise, for what will be revealed. Joseph is a Banyarwanda Hutu, and Cap, a Tetela, an ethnic Bantu. Cap considers himself a true Congolese, his people comes from the heart of the country. For centuries they lived of the Lomami River, farmed cassava, bananas and kola nuts. He is no stranger to hard work and sacrifice, and, quite adept in living off the land. The tribal system in the Congo is very complex to say the least, there are many ethnic groups, sub-groups and categories. Many alliances have been formed in the past, as it mattered for physical survival. But now much so for convenience, and economic survival.

Joseph links with the Ugandan officer was confirmed by Cap. As it turned out, he is his distant cousin. Not all of the men were armed. They met every few days at Joseph camp, which was closer to the drop-off point. They would weigh what they found, calculate returns and plan for the week ahead. Business was going good, Cap added workers as his mine expanded. He brought in almost twice as Joseph did, which was never acknowledged.

Joseph armed the villagers that worked for him, by then

have gotten his confidence. They were strong, he could rely on them, not rag-tagged and weak. Cap, Leo, and his former soldiers were armed, but not his villagers. They were not trained Cap thought, they cannot friend from foe, distinguish. During the foregone period, allegiances were built, as the men would look up to their two leaders, the dystopian society they created. The 'master' for Joseph. But a genuine leader of men, Cap wanted most of all to be seen as such, respected. Unlike Joseph who relished the 'god like' syndrome, of being looked upon, and the patronage he offers, to those who have done.

A time for much grief and pain, the middle of the following year, it would emerge in their relationship…that 'stain'. The feelings that Joseph harboured towards his friend, of envy bordering disdain. That a trivial disagreement, would lead him to say: 'I would shoot you in the head' if you were someone else, haunts Cap to the present day. Bewildering, he did not see this coming. What could provoke such animosity? The hate in his voice, and what he said so…callously.

Overlooked at the time, Cap ill-prophesised, this is how he is. 'I would not read too much into this'. Joseph is both senior in age and rank, Cap however, displayed qualities as such that he did not. Even the Colonel recognised the intelligence and leadership Cap always displayed, as he would comment the times they met, you are my brother, with Joseph did not sit well. His fear of being replaced by Cap as he felt, was being realised. Evidenced by the natural appeal Cap has with others, especially his own cousin, worried him.

In his mind, Joseph that is, would start to create, conditions that would breed hate. Hate for the other, Cap in the present matter. To conceal his failures, he would blame, those who unwittingly would add to his shame. So it came to a head one day at Joseph's camp, laid bare for all to survey. Could not believe their eyes, as weapons were drawn on Joseph's side. You want everything for yourself, Joseph said to Cap. There were disagreements before about how they should share, either equal or in part, the rewards as they compare.

A non-performer and usurper Joseph was. Unable to match the skills and success of the other, would claim as his own. Not a shot was fired, but it signalled an end, years of friendship and brotherhood, a journey that would end, caused by the greed and bitterness. That conditions so created only in Joseph's mind. The resentment he has harboured towards the other through the years. Cap would realise, all stems from Joseph's failure to achieve anything for himself. As he said to Leo, his one remaining friend, this is the end. I cannot trust him anymore, we must split and go alone, but, must prepare to defend.

We do not need him, we can make enough for us to succeed. We will continue dealing with the Colonel, this has nothing to do with him, and neither should care. Cap was not afraid of Joseph, but elicited from Leo, his unwilling participation in sending the message. He did not want to make matters worse, knowing of Joseph's irrational and unpredictable nature, decided that this would be the best course of action. A direct confrontation would be worse, not better.

But the result of, and unforetold reaction, would bring to the fore, years of mounting aggression. With an ominous smile, "I will do what I must", was his reply. It was all that Joseph would say, to the message that was sent. In a strange way, Joseph still loved his old friend, but wanted to see him destroyed financially, reduced to nought, crippled in other words. He wanted him to feel pain, but did not know how, to carry out such a wicked plot. He has felt shunned in the presence of Cap for so long, for it was time to take the stage he thought, 'destroy him, I am better, think he is great'.

Joseph has built over the previous time, a reputation of brutality, how he dealt with others. The many he came across when he expanded his mine. The 'warlord' nascent if you will, the epithet he always wanted, the fear and the cringe. He has sown the seeds of mistrust among his men…now so dread, towards Cap and those that he led. We will destroy what they have built, and they will come crawling. We would attack his camp at night, cause disarray, but not to kill them. We will burn his house down, the one he has made, for his family 'so precious', they would pay.

That he would disregard the years of friendship, and all I have I done, helped him through the tough times, when he had no one. It was all about Cap, in Joseph's head, never about them, and the mischief he would spread. To create chaos, and take the mine, not to kill, but wipe out all they he could find. What he built, for Cap to have nothing left, in his mind, was better than this feeling that consumes him all the time.

That for which he could never live up, the standards that Cap set. For one modicum of thought would have lifted him up, to that place he wanted to be, next to, or even above the one, he so envied. He would never admit, it was greed all the time. To have more than the other, especially for him, would design. A plot once and for all, to eliminate the legacy, the memory of long felt inferiority.

He set fire to the house that night, where his family slept. He did to run them out, but they perished instead. The wooden structure could not withstand, engulfed in flames collapsed around them. Trapped they died…

…Unwitting actors, in the game of envy, greed, and pride.

The attack on the camp was abandoned, when he realised what just happened. The deaths he did not intend, and, the fear of revenge, he would have to disappear then. The loss of his two children and his wife, for which he had worked so hard, to give a better life. For him too much to bear, having lost all that he held dear. Joseph with his men would disappear into the wilderness. Cap vowed to avenge, the loss of his family, for the treacherous act, Joseph would pay.

Security and the freedom from fear, is but an illusion in this…the Basin. Matters you must, take into your hands, acts of injustice and violence perpetrated. Retribution is up to you, absent is the law of the land, and those who seek…only shall find. There is no one to turn to, when wrong is done to you. What else is there, it is what they created. Conditions for the strong to survive, the weak to suffer, prey on those and you shall prosper. In this the land of injustice and now anger. Cap would hunt night and day, for Joseph his friend and those who betray. Months gone by, unable to find, he would return one day. For in his mind, revenge is not a dish that gets cold, but grows hotter in time.

Back to square one, Cap would now relocate his operation to a safer place. Hundreds of mile to the south, away from the carnage and chaos, the conflict now erupting, The Kivus were no longer safe, the Second War saw major shifts, migration flows and skirmishes. Acts of violence and intimidation, human rights gone out the window, absolute suffering only to follow. Vengeance, repression, greed and retribution, are synonymous with this war, as never seen before.

Even the first have never seen this magnitude. Of hunger and distress, with cruelty they would repress. Those whose dignity, cannot defend, against the barbarity and atrocity, the lords would oversee. They are but collateral damage, they say, but pawns they are, in this vicious game of superiority, on display. Die they must, we will prove our right, with inhumanity and all our might.

The wars in The Congo, is all but to follow. A history of cruelty and oppression, of sadistic violence that would create the condition. Conditions, all that they know, for non-other did they bestow. Examples set by the masters before, would leave a legacy for them to follow.

Copy they did, as the masters insist, for docility…those who resist. Chop off their hand, or their head, in this state of savagery…and bloodshed. For none have foretold what better life await, in the absence of war and inherent 'hate'. They had not a glimpse of what would seem. What a normal life would be like, for their children… a fulfilled dream.

The milieu, the conditions, the Kivus is home to, not one or two, but dozens. Armed groups of many sizes, aligned and not, the countries east…bequeath. Patronage some would reap, for The Congo army they would keep, in their favour, but when it is over, would align with another. In the acronyms, sometimes hard to discover. True allegiance a myth, it is no wonder, many are betrayed in this cycle of conflict, and plunder.

As the militias unite to protect the innocents, would form alliances with the many villages. Protect them they would, prey on others if they could. Bandits would many turn out to be, to the conflict would add chaos and intractability.

'Rebels' they identify, 'armed groups' we say. 'Thugs' they

are called for whom they prey. Elites would form and unite, support those for them can provide, the backing they need, to satisfy their greed.

Usurp the power of the army commander, the competition, the resources for which, we can do better. Enmeshed in violence, the Eastern Congo hotbed of resistance, and, the resistance they have championed, from the slave trade to colonial repression.

In the nineties, to democratise, ethnic violence they would mobilise. It is about resistance, and to those who would function, to dictate terms of their...inheritance.

History of chaos

Independence would bring, a new dispensation of rivalry and bickering. Centrism, one they would fight, against the West the other would unite. Divisions no longer concealed, sprung forth, constituencies. Ethnically charged and align...set forth upon democracy, for they have embarked, on downward spirals' reign of anarchy.

It remains today, the contest for decay. Ethnic competition and social fragmentation, the battle to annihilate, masked with the cover of ethnic hate. For conflict is a symptom of, not a cause, of unresolved issues, and only because. Fool themselves they may, the reasons concealed, they hope would stay.

By contest could not replace, overthrow then, the reins of government Mobuto would take. Would crush the violence in the Kivus proper, for there remains pockets of resistance along the Ugandan border. Mobuto would emerge, victory over those...he would purge. With the help of friends and paid soldiers, America would pitch in with jet fighters.

A one party state he did create, of patronage and presidential dictate. By this he would secure, peace in the Kivus, but just to make sure. Rule with iron fist, the force apparatus, quash rebellion and quell dissenters.

Dwindling resources he was sure. The end of the Cold War brought nothing more. His American friends can no longer rely, true democracy let us give it a try.

Mobuto would work behind the scenes.
Divide and conquer, stoke ethnic fervour.
Banned political groups and stifled the process.
Militias they formed, the political parties 'reformed'.
Mobuto ensured by 'existential' blunder.
The nascent democracy shall remain asunder.

He too would fall, as the democratic process…he did forestall.
The conditions he did create, lived by the bullet…fled from it.

Chapter Five

Wars, Uncommon

One

There were conflicts.
Based on self-determination.
Independence, ideology, and revolution.

But in the nineties.
After the Cold War.
The Phenomenon would emerge.
Brought to the fore.

Not of inter-state rivalries.
As the decades before.

Post-colonial separation.
Democracy, and communism.

Outdated, defunct, now gone.
But among people, intra-state.
The new, one.

The conflicts manifest.
Of unresolved differences.

And in Africa.
Minerals they contest.

In Europe East.
They would create.
Soviet's lust for land.
They did appropriate.

Left for all, after.
Communism, the fall.

The condition, disintegration.
The carnage, ethnic divide.
Fragmentation.

In Africa, it will be replete.
The fall of Somalia, in the east.

The genocide in Rwanda, the centre.
In Liberia, the west.
And, Sierra Leone, their neighbour.

New wars, not old ones.
Of track tops and jeans.
Not army fatigues, greens.

Indiscipline, chaos.
The drugged out heads of child soldiers.

Placed on the, frontline.
The elites stand, behind.

Battle they would, for loot.
Close their eyes, they shoot.

Fall they may.
Brother, sister.
Father, mother.

Forced, to kill.
Turn you, into monster.

The atrocities apparent.
The disease inherent.

Born and bred.
In violence, they stand.
The conditions, now demand.

Two

The Nations United.
Did not grasp.
The magnitude, severity.
The new wars.
They would, lapse.

The shame.
The embarrassment.
The genocides.
They could not, prevent.

Their hands, tied.
Their mandates, defied.

Words on paper.
They are played.
Duped and bound.
Await the warlord's.
Second round.

The catch-up, the game.
Anticipate not, for it is about.
What has, been done?
What can, be proven?

Wars has always been about.
The belligerence of nations.

Not, ethnic.
Tribal, relations.

For, so long.
They have been stuck.
The game of militarism.
In this, the complex globalism.

The complex, they worship.
For it is about profit.

Not feed the poor.
Settle their disputes.
For their lives, secure.

Sell weapons, instead.
Gun running, for sure.

The nations, would sell.
Some on the Council, as well.

Land mines and prohibited weaponry.
Designed to kill, as much of the enemy.

In a sense, it has never been.
About world peace, and less suffering.

The United Nations would design
Plan unique, even they, cannot malign.

The Responsibility, they said.
For you, To Protect.
Your people, so reliant.

Usurp we will, your duties.
If you are, defiant.

As previously, all fail.
This too, shall not prevail.

Our friend, the dictator.
Council Members, would not falter.

Support them, our friends.
Syria and Sudan proper.

Suffer him, who has no other.
The pariah, the mad dog of Africa.

For years of tyranny.
He would pay.
Betrayal mostly.
France would lead, the way.

The stray he was.
Put down, he must.
He reminded, of.

Three

Almost a decade, would past.
In this new era, it did last.

Warfare, not seen before.
Ethnic hatred, insurmountable greed
That would, trigger it.

Diplomacy.
And the Rule of Law.
Outlandish notions in.
The Cold War's thaw.

Nations bent, and defied.
The supremacy of the UN.
They once relied.

Accede, they did.
It mattered, then.

The contest of nations.
The hegemony, the strength.

The Cold War.
Could not, defend.

The rise of nations.
Would usher a new dispensation.

Hands untied, the power reveal.
The countries, long suffered.
The superpower, appeal.

Go their own, make their way.
UN, the rubber stamp.
For the Council, we say.

Humanitarian, they remain.
Pick up pieces and make better.
What we have broken.
In our quest, for power.

Ideologues, have gone.
The powers, remain.
Many more now.
Too much, to restrain.

The sovereign.
The Westphalian, system
Would be our right.
On which, we bargain.

Protect us, you must.
As we sow the seeds, chaos.

Protect us, from those.
Who would intervene?
To help the innocents.
Or so, it would seem.

Disguised always.
Never realistic.
What is gracious, kind?
Never altruistic.

The United Nations.
The design.
Vestige of, global war.
Nuclear proliferation.

Would have to adapt.
Think on its feet, reactive.
Challenges, unheard.
Unseen, proactive.

Four

Who would have known, even thought.
Humanity would be reduced.
To less than nought.

The conditions, unliveable.
The slaughter, the hate.
The genocide, create.

The complex web, deprivation and war.
The cycle that takes, more and more.

Civil, it never was.
Brutal and barbarous.
Among people that lived.
As neighbours.

What can evoke such atrocity?
Animosity, not even.
Among strangers, enemy?

For years they live.
Signs of accord.
Forget not the past.
The elites, sow discord.

We say intra-state conflict, now.
The neologism, euphemism
Political correctness, somehow.

Scholars they try.
Explain this conflict, they rely.

The one, the few outdated notions.
It is political they say.
Social fragmentation or repression.

Greed or grievance.
Must be one or the other.
Cannot be the two.
So, do not bother.

The question we have grappled.
As we have asked ourselves.
What gave rise?
To this state of affairs?

That, which gave rise.
We refuse to accept.
That which causes.
Upheaval and revolution.
Sometimes, the inept.

Of those, removed from power.
The dictator, immersed.
In his own, splendour.

In Cuba, in Iran.
Not Gadhafi.
For we now know, the plan.

Ben Ali and Mubarak.
The Spring Season, did upset.

Suffer they did.
Years of tyranny.
Poverty and Neglect.

Mothers they weep.
Their children go hungry.

It is all about hunger.
As desperation takes over.
For no one fights.
If their bellies are full.

> *Provide for your people…ensure.*
> *They remain loyal to you.*
> *Matters not…if impure.*

Five

Conflicts manifest.
In a box, it would not rest.
Reveal it must.
The ugly truth.
Incongruous distrust.

The disdain.
Those who keep you under.
Feelings could not restrain.
The Intifada.

Shaking off, they say.
Hamas, the Authority.
Would pay.

Years, they use.
Their own people
Their suffering.
Now recuse.
Blame, the Jews.

No conflict of interest.
Israel, created.
Palestinians, perpetuated.

The conditions rife.
For suffering and strife.

In one form, or another.
In every era.
Conflicts are revealed.
Cannot stay, under.

Radical alterity.
Subversive tendency.
React, accordingly.
Bring down, completely.

Today, conflict designed.
Attack not from outside.
But from, inside.

Bring down, governments.
Bring down, the state.
The seed, of hate.
As negligence dictate.

Stoke unrest.
The people who detest.
Their leaders, deny.

Human dignity, human rights.
Free from fear.
The future.
Secure, near.

Political participation.
We may not, care.

We leave, to you.
In your hands.
Our future, our children.
Our destiny, completely.

Gamble they will.
The spoils fulfil.
Their needs extravagant.
Their ego hubristic.
The mental opulent.

Six

Intra-state conflict.
The new, war.
The conditions, the need.
For this, to succeed.

Relies on many elements.
Factors on the ground.
Political instability.
The vacuum created.
The absence of Security.
…Poverty.

> *'The hope of a better life, glimmer sufficient'*
> *Is all it takes, to reduce the chances!*
> *For the many factors, it negates.*
> *Rather than, enhances!*

The negativity.
The absence of Human Security.
For people.
Not country.

People's needs to survive.
To prosper and thrive.
Education, for their children.
Their health, a better nation.

Employment.
Provide for themselves.

To live in freedom not fear.
The state apparatus.
The forced disappearance.

The knock.
The door, at night.
The anticipation.
The terror, the fright.

Decide, their fate.
By the ballot box, create.
Democracy, for all.
Not, dictatorship.
Anocracy they fall.

Zimbabwe's, Mugabe.
Sudan's, al Bashir.
Had created, such.
Uncertain atmosphere.

Gone but not forgotten.
Remnants remain.

Their memory.
Their legacy.
Ill-gotten.

> *Never, again.*
> *Indelible, the stain.*
> *Scarred psyche.*
> *The people, retain.*

Chapter Six

The Conversation, Part One

Patrice would begin to pick up from Cap, more about his life story. What led him to this unforgiving place, and the reasons for working so hard? Why he has been pushing him as a young man to become stronger and more resilient. Conditioning him in a sense, for some unseen trial in his future life. Patrice like a sponge is soaking up everything, he is at that age, wanting to learn anything. Like some kind of history lesson begins with his own life's story. Patrice in his curious mind starts to unravel the details about the man he now looks up to like a father.

Unintended it may be, they both see in each other qualities they hoped to find in a father, and a son. Cap's monologue takes place late evenings when they have all retired, in his shelter not too far from Patrice's and the other kids. Most of the other children has been taken in by the families who work in the mines. A few of them have disappeared along with the families that looked after them. The conditions are difficult, especially during the rainy season. The work is hard and backbreaking. But, they are not treated like slaves, beaten, or abused. But, pushed constantly, as if on a schedule.

Each family share a makeshift tent, Patrice with Maurice

and Dalia. The men have constructed two gender specific enclosed pit latrines. Ensuring some privacy and sanitation at least. They now fetch water and bathe upstream away from the mine. It is better the children would think at times. Not having to fend for themselves, on the streets of the slums.

The children did not get the family Leo had promised. But ended up in a 'community' that looked out for each other. Patrice still has his brother, now a sister, and much better, someone he can look up to, a father figure. Cap is the perfect father, in Patrice's mind. He was built strong, tough, he is intelligent, always reading. Patrice would always notice Cap intently thinking, before he says or does anything. He does not know his real father, and honestly does not care anymore about that.

He remembers his mother, her warm smile and loving touch. He thinks about Loraine and Mama Nieve, he left without telling them anything. They must be worried, and would be disappointed to know what he has done. In the back of his mind, he knows he will make it up to them.

The interaction between Cap and Patrice, the one they have on evenings. Can be described more as directions and instructions, rather than a conversation. Lessons passed down from one generation to another. Father to son, or elder to... younger one.

They are both from the same tribe, which for them made the process natural. In one sense, Cap thinks, he was fulfilling his duty as a responsible adult. To convey lessons learnt, to the next generation.

For Patrice in another, as a child would learn from a father. After a simple, but warm dinner, after all have retired to their tents. Patrice would sit with Cap outside his, where it begins.

The stridulating crickets adds tempo to the discourse.

Broken only by the howl and screech, that comes from the forest floor within…reach.

As the master to his student, the tenets of life conveyed intricately, sometimes hidden, mostly bluntly, in the stories told… begotten.

I have lost mine, then who am I?
For the one who I have now, found
Unable to give, to pass on.

The lessons of my life, my suffering, what I was denied.
For you are no one, if none to teach, none to give.
All you have built in life, matters not, if just, memories.

Wealth not, for this can be taken away.
I would give to this child, this boy, my son adopted.
My legacy, the one that would stay, never to be forgotten.

This is the first lesson to you.
Harshly he begins, understand, you are nothing.
No one cares, whether you perish or survive.
No one, whether in this country, or elsewhere.
Knows you are alive.

You must make yourself someone first.
You are just another, African child.
Until you make yourself special, 'standout' if you will.

Littered in this land, the remains.
Those, who considered themselves great.
Leaders, the generals, the fighters.

None have survived, to tell the tale.
Show the way, out of this pit.
This grave, this hell-hole, we occupy.

Life means nothing in this place.
One day you are here.
Next you are gone, and no one cares.
You are a number, just a statistic.

My family, taken years ago.
Murdered by someone, I know.
A brother to me.
My boy would have been your age now.
My daughter was then, three.

I have no one left in this world.
My lovely wife, children, all gone.
Their lives snatched, taken away from me.

Fleeting is life, by the ravages of war, barely few survive.
Those destined, will make a difference.
Wanting nothing more…

…the guilt to be alive.
Teach others, make a difference.
For nothing left…life is meaningless.

It is my duty to inform you, get you ready for what lies ahead.
The rigours of life, things you need to know, to survive. Never get
too comfortable, 'bad things' happen when you get complacent.
It breeds neglect, I learnt this the hard way…with regret.

I will not teach you the ways of death, for this consumes the mind, learn about politics and war instead. Find your centre, your destiny, it may not happen now, before you know it, it is the source, it is all you see.

We are all born with the desire to achieve something.
For some, greater than expected.

I see in you the urge, the need to prove yourself. This must be tempered by learning and patience…to be respected. You are intelligent, bright, and capable of anything. Learn about what would make this country better…

…a leader, maybe, this is your calling.

I will teach you about the war, our mistakes. What we did wrong and the troubles we have made. What we caused, about loss, the sins of men. The degeneration of war, why people kill, why soldiers and rebels rape. About poverty and getting rich.

The struggle to survive.
Why we bring down each other.
Things we do, the desperation to stay alive.

We are destined to make the same mistakes.
We treat others, as we are treated.
A rehash of history, it is repeated.

In a never ending cycle of poverty, destruction, oblivion.

Why it is important, to get out of poverty.
This I tell you, 'our' problem.

We are poor, we were born this way.
And so shall we, remain.
Unless we figure out, a better way.

The secret my boy, is education.
This is hope for the future, not the past.
For history only gives reasons, lessons.
But education, prospects for a better day.

What we have accumulated
The wealth taken from this land.
We did not create, cannot replace it.

We must learn from the past, never repeat.

Inglorious is war, never mind what you have been told.
Victory comes at a price, what was held before.
We can no longer hold, anymore.

We think about those we have lost.
At night they come calling.
Wake you from sweaty dreams.
When you are at the edge of that cliff.
Before you start falling.

They come in this time, of need.
Sad, you were not there, when they plead.
Loss, is all that comes to mind.
Relish never the fortunes, means nothing.

Like written words, lost to the blind.
Spoken words, lost in time.

Conditions Created

One

Understand, it is 'not' about hate.
We love our African brothers, our sisters.
It is only that, we create.
What is required, that mental state.

Subject to and conducive, to take from each other.
And, from our mother, the bounties she offers.

Like those came before, our forefathers.
Written in blood, the generations before.
History be 'told, no better way of wealth, secure.

To prosper, you must keep under.
Those who may rival, we vanquish forever.

We find ways, to see in the 'other'.
Reasons to hate, tribal, religious.
But this is only, a cover.

Feelings we have, of deprivation.
The denial of justice, we suffer.
We take out on 'their' own, kindred brother.

The aggression, formed by a lifetime of oppression.

For it is after all, but a competition.
We compete, for food.
We compete, to survive.
Compete for the resources.
For the riches, this land so divides.

The conditions, which we live.
Have grown, accustomed.
The struggles, besieged.

The 'ties' that could bind, would never dictate.
The 'unanimity' we crave.
It has never been, never created.
'Machinations' of those.
Who would keep us, separated?

Generations have come.
Have gone, still they divide.
The people, they linger, they are torn.
By the ethnic war, they provide.

Suffer thy nation.
The multitudes, dying men
Starving children.
The wailing, women.

War made us.
We were born, bred.

In this, conflicted land.
For the many generations, have spanned.

Has brought only suffering, chaos.
Solutions never to be had, never at hand.

Destitute surely, in this place.
We still stand.

Two

Poverty is the requirement, this I say.
It made me what I am today.
And so it would to you.

Survive it you must.
Or, be reduced to the heap.
Of those who have used.
For their lives, incomplete.

In poverty we were born.
It is what we…re-create.
The needless violence.
The destruction regress.
Assuredly poverty, the mind-set.

Notion dispel, the truth repel.
Palliative the disease.
The innocence, we plead.

The hand, we were dealt.
To…survive.
The choices we make
Repercussions, long felt.

Blame the state, blame the government.
Shame on the colonisers, shame on the forbearers.
We blame not, the ones, cause the rot.
Ignore them we say, this we must not.

Decades gone, still cannot adjust.
Hundred years, time have past.
The legacy, colonisation.
Still cripples, imagination.

Brutal dictator, freedom fighter, now usurper.
Caught in a timeless warp, in minds they create.
Conjure they would, the conviction, the falsehood.

Independent they say
Freedom of choice.
For it is, never about.

Dissent create, the ballot obfuscate.
The conditions remain, cannot get out.
Mired the cycle, self-doubt.

What to do, no choice.
Continue we will
The timeless journey.
For our lives still, to fulfil.

What has been made, given us?
The patrimony.
The required state.
Desired…mistrust.

They have not, would never create.
The conditions we need.
For our dreams, remains incomplete.

Keep us poor.
Keep us in hell.
Prey on us, they ensure.
Remain in power, cherish the loot.
Suffer, thy brother…

> *…slow descent.*
> *Feels like…forever.*

Hopes and aspirations

One

My boy, forget not your dreams.
This is what they want.
So it seems.

Never give up hope.
Hope for a better life.
In the struggle and the scrape.
The mind is fully utilised.

Focus you must, only the matters at hand.
Eat once a day, survive if you can.

May never realise, your full potential.

From birth caught
The bird' wing'ed, clipped.
Fly never, trapped forever.

So you are, remain inside looking out.
Release the mind, let it seek, it shall find.

Thoughts they progress, dreams limitless.
Adaptation the key, fruition, completely.

Be told you will, give up dreams.
The hope they remove, not instil.

Want better, not more.
Greed consumes, does not endure.

Dreams fade, when hope is lost.
Dysfunction the key that makes the cost.

What to do, you may wonder.
Caught you are.
But trapped, not forever.

Imagine a life better than this.
This you can do, just live it.

Pretend you are somewhere else.
That place you want to be.
Will get you there…

…with hope, achieve your dreams.

Find it, the cracks and the spaces.
From the few that are kind, the traces.

Hope carries you, most important.
Without, everything is irrelevant.

Hope fades, like the sundown.
Depressed you feel, when it is gone.

Will rise again, before you know.
The warmth it brings, fills from head to toe.

'Never…give up'
'Never say…die'
'Never…give up'

This mantra repeat.
Keep it alive, eventually.
It will be, complete.

Two

I was on my way
Equipped only.
My hopes and dreams
Did not sway.

Carried me, most difficult times.
When all was lost, so I thought.
What I could find.

Rekindle the desire, rekindle the drive.
Found always, the inspiration.
That which connects.
Reality and imagination.

Thoughts fulfil, what is not.
Imagery, the manifestation.
That brings about.

Obstacles, they throw in my direction.
Confusion, they cause, the reaction.

Flinch I did, the second or so.
Picked up always, on my way did…go.

Challenges in life, I did confront.
Transformation, easy for me.
…Necessary.

Keep me down, some they try.
Others did not, on me rely.
Unique you are, some see…indispensability.
For some a threat, I was not.
Who knows the key…manoeuvrability?

In the least, a challenge.
I am honest with myself.
By this, I manage.

The issues I faced, you will too.
Inherent they remain.
Challenges cannot deny…refrain.

Accept them we must.
Find ways to defeat.
Incomparable, some may be.
Insurmountable, you give up.
…Completely.

Find the will, your inner drive, climb that hill…stay alive.

Problems confront
One by one, they amount.
Dealt I did, the issues in front.

Worry never.
Which confound.
Inability…propound.

Many a great men, have told.
For those we extol.
The virtues of discretion
Patience…forbearance.

Solutions come, answer they will.
Questions, long puzzled, our existence.

Shocked you will discover.
Not alone, do we suffer.

What makes you different, get you out.
The succession, that keeps all under.

The immanent desire
Make yourself great at any cost.
The legacy you create.
They will follow…admire.

Chapter Seven

The Conversation, Part Two

It is important for you to know, as a child.
Details you may not understand, as to what and why?
You will later, but for now, just an idea.

What plagues this land, the wars we see and experience?
Brings suffering, pain and misery.
Dauntless we face, the many, an eternity.

The generations, those taken.
Remain, lost, forgotten.
Never understand.
But see, the face of death.
Still visits this land.

Blackened, sky fills, clouds gather.
We look, silver lining do not favour.

No hope, no brighter day.
The sun on Africa, sets.
The darkness, the continent.

Look to the East, we do.
The sun rises.
But brings war, turmoil.
Resplendent the blood, spills on, soil.

Conflicts crafty like men.
Designed, hide.
True motives, intentions.
Leaders, malign-ed.

Deadly the ground, they play.
Game of chess, joust.
King, queen, topple…not.
But the many pawns, they slay.

> *The price…we pay.*
> *Resource…the curse.*
> *Interlocutors…emerge.*
> *Interlopers…the purse.*

First War

The seed, this conflict.
Decades ago planted.
Long before, the General pursue.
The Hutu, supplanted.

The peasants, immigrant population.
Refugees, borders, the problem.

Conditions were right.
Chaos, he creates.
Armed intervention, disunite.

Ethnic allegiance, revert.
Animosities, re-emerge.

> *The conflict results…complex would be.*
> *The 'First War of Africa'*
> *Voila…enmity*
> *Ala…Kigame.*

A bust for him. …Boon for them
Pursue their enemies.
The many countries would, their armies.

Mobuto's blessing did not need, seek.
Enter Zaire, create, havoc.
Rid his foes, the process his luck.

A thorn on the side, he was.
Western powers, await results.

All fell down, home return.
Come back some, over and over.
Militias they are, rebellion they favour.

The Tutsi.
Give up…never.
Vestige of Hutu…genocide.
Slaughter.

Second War

My boy, this war never ended.
Remnants remained, even blended.

One

Lusaka Accord, Peace
Only a reprieve.
Solved nothing.
But weariness and fatigue.

Chance to regroup
Comeback swinging.
Much more than the first.
Vengeance now, they thirst.

Finish, what they started.
Congo, the break-up,
They hastily, departed.

Double crossing, assassinations, murder.
Hollywood scenes, spectacular.

This…the 'Continental War'.
The Kivus, the spark.
Catalytic…apocalyptic.

Would bring down, all.
Monumental, they fall.

Every country, East, West, North, South.
Would have a hand.
'Piece' they want, of this land.

Adventurism, greed.
Dwindling economies.
The…need.

Turning tides, approbation over.
Kabila holds on tight to power.

Try once and again
Assassinate, in vain.

Rwanda, Uganda, stoke confrontation.
Support rebellion…insurgence.

Zimbabwe, Angola, Kabila they support, major.
Sudan a little, Mobuto once.
Now they favour.

Alliances, proxies, unbridled mix-up.
Devastating consequences, the mis-hap.

Two

Not in far fields, they fight.
Confrontations long ago, they might.

Gone, the old war.
Gentlemen like, gallantry.
Welcome the new.
Cower behind, the peasantry.

In towns and villages
Remote, isolated places.
Unfettering, punitive, amusing…wry.
Destroy mud, straw huts.
Houses burnt, the battle…cry.

The soldiers.
Many forces, rebels alike.
Does not distinguish.
Rape those who show allegiance.
…Appearance.

Casualty, collateral damage.
Weapon of war.
Sullied…belligerence.

Ignominious, they instil…fill.
Bring fear, pain, loathing…remain.
The scars, shame.
Mutilation…inflict.
Unwanted…pregnancies.

'Your' spoils…conflict.

People…escape.
Run some would.
Forest deep, shelter seek.

A babe in arms.
Clothes on back.
Pot or pan.
Seep a rice sack.

Displaced, they be.
Drive out completely…key.
Ethnic cleansing, rape…murder.
Pogrom…deliver.

> *Genocide…do not mention,*
> *'Community' never agree.*
> *The bar, higher standard.*
> *What does it take?*
> *Confront…the pernicious…atrocious.*
> *Attritious, downward spiral.*
> *Descent into…calamity.*
> *Rwanda…abruptly?*

Cause and Peace

'Peace…'
Not in this land
Never cared, no one does.
What would it mean?
Never…seen.

Remarkable, would be.
The sight, 'No' sound.
Gunshots…ring.
People…cry out.

A normal life, anything without.
That, which spilled out.
Pandora's…Box.

Opened up, evils came out.
Intended not, even shout.

How else, this suffering, come about.
The sins of men, create, release.
Pent…primordial…hate.

Peace we crave, none they gave.
Violence instead.
Division, confrontation.
Social exclusion, disassociation.

We…and the others.
Not we…brothers.

Marginalisation, mistrust.
Favouritism…disgust.
Deny…demean.
Reject the scheme.

Suffer they must.
For a time long ago.
Done to…us.

> *'Luckily' they remind.*
> *Our…elites.*
> *Dear leaders…inclined.*
>
> *…Instrumentalisation.*
> *They hold…the key*
> *Release…the possibility.*
>
> *…Constructionism.*
> *Create…ethnic polarisation.*
>
> *Band of brothers…ferment.*
> *…Fragmentation.*

Re-invent…revive hate.
…Fractionalisation.
Necessitate.

Positive peace, never.
Negative peace.
Even a sliver.

Desperately, seek.
Future generations, need.
Conditions, the signs bleak.
Denude of possibilities.

Hapless, confront sensibilities.
Build…peace.
Solutions, belie expectations.
Many would try, the Nations.
I.N.G.O. only…salutations.

The Force, Intervention Brigade.
Eliminate with haste, rebel departure.
Concurrent should desire.
Deconstruct proxy, they conspire.

Live to fight another day.
Re-invent, intervene.
Re-create another…scene.

Like plastered, opened sore.
Symptoms treat, source ignore.
Never re-treat, fools' panacea…deceit.

Allocate blame.
Not velvet gloves handle.
Those who cause problems.
In Congo affairs meddle.

Sordid, contemptuous.
Statesman unlikely.
The West line up.
Shower praises...blindly.

They all know the cause, the source.
Interference, proxy involvement.

The countries...East.
Unrelentingly feed...the 'beast'.
The bringer, hunger, disease...death.
Scourge they deny, no 'regret'.

> *Neighbours not, those who look out.*
> *Your welfare, their concern.*
> *Never...applied.*
> *Never...felt.*

Now you know.
Understand you should, better.
If you want to be a leader.

Conditions you must create.
A clean slate...manufacture.
Task yourself, purpose effectuate.
Creatively aspire.

Help bring about normality.
Semblance of peace, the feasibility.
Prospects for settlement…dispute.
Land they fight…repute.

Alleviate, ethnic tension.
Bring about changes.
Land reform, legislation.

Source of contempt.
Displacement, fuelled hate.
Landless they fight, ethnic divide.
Revanche…the tide.

Nothing to lose, no need to hide.
Outright open hostility.
Scorched…annihilate…policy.

Generations, upon itself.
Inherent morbid, revulsion, repulsion.

No fault, all they suffer.
History…elites…created.

The people discarded.
'Melancholic' lost…hope.
Dreams…the departed.

Intense…feelings of doom.
Calamitous…despair.

Lacklustre…desensitised.
Thoughts…mind…impair.

Retreat…fate…await.
Bow…out…resign.

'Leaders' welcome…conviction strong…design.
'Reverse' …historic…wrong…repair.

What it takes, the many intricacies.
Would add to the cause.
Back of your head, keep.

Leaders align, company you seek.
Progressive must be.
Change landscape, completely.

Never…revert.
Digress…inert.

The course, must follow.
Stability, normality…tomorrow.

Reconciliation, relinquish the past.
The pain of forgiveness.
The healing, lasts.

None have displayed.
The fortitude, stamina…grit.
The mantle on, to take.
Formidable requirement.

Superb intellect…wit.

Journey…uncharted territory…make.

Many made the mistake.
Barbaric, primitive.
Solve dispute, by bullet.

Violence, intersessional warfare, beget.
Troubled not, return.
Solutions…doubt.
Did not bring about.
…Peace.

Evanescent…seasonal.
Time it brings relief, solace.
…Occasional.

Winds that shift…agendum create…lift.
Drift…Peace fleeting…shape…Détente.
Minds aligned…create.
Rapprochement…
…Obviate.

Remove chances, flare-ups…advances.
Create condition, roadmap to peace…region.
West align, South North…fine.
Central East, 'relations' must define.
Impertinence, insecurity…the crime.

Transnational…not worry
Terrorism's…understudy.
More than…hard bargain.
Conditions…kept.
…'Flourish'
…'Fragility'
By which…it leapt.

Chapter Eight

Dreams Create, Part One

Patrice would emerge as the main beneficiary, of Cap's growing introspection, he never doubted Cap's intentions. The preceding years was sufficient, he thought. Cap proved himself as someone who truly cares, someone to trust. It is remarkable for someone like Patrice. Who has grown up in poverty, has known this condition all his life. To experience at the same time, unconditional generosity, from the slums to the mine. Something that could only be given by someone, one who has experienced the same hardships? Patrice has come to expect this from the man, he respects tremendously.

His wisdom, Patrice thinks of Cap, seems beyond his years. His remarkable intelligence. His ability to reflect on the past. To use this in the most positive ways to enhance his life, as well as those around him. Seldom would one come across someone like him. Only a fighter, a warrior, can understand peace, what it means, and how to achieve it. And it's value. As one who has been through the trials of life, can only understand poverty. Cap displays qualities found only in great men, Patrice looks up to him.

The role model who emerged from the wilderness.
The most unlikely of places.

Great men, leaders.
Suffer they would.
Lifetime distress, manage could.

Hard lessons, build stronger.
Emerge victorious, far better.

Not faint hearted, confront.
Challenge welcome, surmount.

Build character, oft, problems encounter.
Resilient, pressures withstand, tougher.

Others crumble, dust.
Great men rise, trust.
Take flight, ashes, chaos.

Leader become, the hour.
Pack could not, devour.

See in another, what it takes.
Mind strong, imitate.
Be like me, facilitate.

Build the will, stand apart.
Character develop, instil, impart.

From the moment, Cap laid eyes.
On the one, now his son, it materialised.

Saw in him that spark, that hunger.
Make himself great, like no other.
Cannot let him down, disappoint.

His dream, now mine.
Together, rally cry, will define.

The motive, the agenda.
The condition, I must create.
For it is mine, to make.

Who else, he has no other.
As father must do, for son, daughter.

Great we feel, unable to achieve.
Our children fulfil, what we believe.

Lost dreams, from us escape, clutches.
Grasped, slipped, offspring fingers snatches.
Not given the chance, opportunity.
Put an end, this cycle, imminently.

Fair?
Live dreams…by another.
Surrogate?
Than…nothing
Better?

It has been on his mind for some time. Cap questions himself, why continue operating the mine. This was really a small venture, he thought temporarily. Initially to raise enough money, to start a legitimate company. There is no future in mining, much less by illegal means. The region has become saturated with miners, driven by the demand for coltan. Dangers come in all forms. No longer are mines within the ambits of ex-soldiers like him, or, former rebels. But, now growing criminal enterprises. Other types of mining, as well as illegal logging adds further complications, and dangers. Unintentional encroachment are always possible when scouring for sites. There is no honour with these batches of men, Cap thinks. The landscape is way too dangerous to operate, especially, with the children around him.

Leo has stood with Cap through many trials. Never any good times, there was never any. He also senses that change is needed, they must move on. He will continue to follow his friend, his leader, his Captain, in his decision making. Just packing up and moving away, is out of the question. Cap needs to come up with a plan. A transition from one phase, conditioned by obstacles and hardship. To another, something better, less burdensome, dangerous, treacherous.

The snake in the tall grass strikes.
Clear path, ahead lies.
Front away, extant, any longer stay.

Cap and Leo have both amassed small fortunes. Cap, always steps ahead, have already planned out his strategy. About a possible future business, and the plans for the children. And, how he was going to deal with the enduring problem 'Joseph'.

Cap has already made arrangements for the three children's education. On his many trips into town, made contact with a small Catholic run home, with the nun. Not an orphanage, but a not for profit paid institution. It has electricity, only intermittently. But does have running water, toilets, baths, and, soft warm beds. Most importantly, hot meals every day. The children surely will be comfortable, would not mind the stay.

Deep in his heart, knows, he has fooled.
For the labour of men, women, children, used.

For his sins, give back, repent.
For his luck, already spent.
Granted no longer.
Make way, time to discover.

New chances, possibility.
Luck we make, create opportunity.

Lead the way.
Self, mobilise.
Children, prioritise.
Workers, subsidise.

Time elapse, make haste.
Not wait, waste.
Adventure await, taste.
New opportunity, tidings gladly.
Momentous, the joy, finally.

Reveal he did, the good news.
The children unable to contain their happiness.
Measure of appreciation, willingness.

Years did take, realise dream.
Father found.
Life, education.
Now future, sound.

Cap and Leo would make a clean break from mining. They handed over the operations to the couple of families that opted to stay. The rest moved on, the squalor and unpredictability. The ups and downs, inclement weather, too much, could not bear, any longer. Many have retired, from ailments related to coltan extraction process.

Migration flows, induced by the demand for labour. Just as that of the internally displaced, caused by conflict, is not uncommon in The Congo. It would therefore not alarm anyone one to see scores of people moving from one place to another. Furthermore, and especially in mining areas. In the subsequent years, following the second war. Reflecting on the events, even more…soul searching. There was an urgency for security and stability.

Painfully, Cap recalls what caused him to leave the Kivus. Honestly, he does not think he is lucky. He misses his family… terribly. Sorrow and guilt consumes him all the time. But maybe, this was his 'destiny' to find these children. To help them fulfil…theirs.

There is anguish, the thought confuses.
His family replaced by orphans, speculates.

Everything happens, in this place.
Happiness, sadness, war, death, rebirth.
Everything is played out here.
The microcosm, heaven, hell, earth.

This land, has the ability to bring out every emotion, facet from one. From brave warrior to forager, now digger. Family man to widower, now utopian. Destiny holder, giver, benefactor, now sponsor.

Indeed this, the plan for me.
Would grab with both hands, firmly.
Thinks, have been better-off, if done for me.
Surely not, a different man, completely.

Upon their arrival, Cap would immediately place into the hands of Sister Beatrix, into her care, Dalia, Marcel and Patrice. The town a bustling place, dangers lurk in all forms, disguises. Unsavoury characters, drug fiends, perverts, and bandits.

Cap was sure, placed in 'her' hands, strict, vigilant, protection ensure. The home 'haven' for safe keeping…secure. For children, parents could not look out for. Education, build values, discipline, health and nutrition. A sense of belonging, part of the system, register their names, birth this place. The crack through slips, prevent, a life delinquent. Add value to community…society…build country.

No place, better start.
That which, evade.
Now become, part.

The children are looked after, needs provided by volunteers, paid a small, but daily stipend. It is better than nothing, most would think, look after these kids. Give back, sense of duty, calling. Almost all the home's guardians, were at one time cared for by the Sister. They all lead productive lives now. Testament to the values instilled, and, stability, the 'Immaculate One' home provides.

By far, not a fancy boarding school.
Libraries, full of books.
Computer lab, swimming pool.
Landscaped green, flowers blossom.
Walkways lined, hedged halcyon.

Surrounded by noise.
The dust that blow.
The street, from which comes.

Behind, thin paned window.
View, know.

All that separates, bad from good.
The short fence, behind.
They play, stood.

Make their way, the many schools.
The Sister, dutifully overlooked.

Decked clean, whitened shoes, they stream.
Out the gate, one by one, coordinate.

Their eyes shun, distractions abate.
Mistake not make, replicate.
Reprobate taunt, the Sister, they placate.

At the gate, Sister stand.
Flock returns, hand in hand.

Their brother, their sister, their keeper.
The sense of family, instil.
Tribal, ethnic, past separate.
The bond, which must now, create.

> *Put an end, on which they depend.*
> *Elites rely, differences rather would…multiply.*

Sister Beatrix, the Blessed Traveller.

The one who voyaged many miles, in search of her destiny, found, ended in Lubumbashi. Born into a wealthy Belgian family. Her ancestors acquired their fortunes, 'directly' from connections with the state. Rubber importation business. Well…precisely.

The Congo, source of riches, would accumulate.
Built on the backs, sweat of the natives.
They prospered, she would postulate.

At an early age, well educated.
Would champion 'the' cause.
Disillusionment, remorse.
Family sins…because.

What she would do, choices limited?
Humanitarian, nascent, blossoming.

Join she would, the 'Church' Catholic.
Provided the backdrop, setting.

Established, well connected.
Hands that reach, all places.

Roots laid, service provided.
Champions, they are
She would, embellish.

Staunch Catholics.
Patrons, the sainted.
Tither, the church.
Requested, granted.

Give up, abandon, all she knows.
Magnificent buildings, hallowed halls.
The comfort, mansion luxurious, wealth affords.

The wide paved streets, Brussels trade.
The dirt roads, pothole sunk
Water filled, Congo rains made.

Would meet, encounter see.
The long perilous, journey, traverse.
The alternate side, this universe.

Will take in stride.
Conscious clear, ready to serve.
Protected feels, driven fearlessly.

> *Canticulum hum, her saviour, praise.*
> *Beneficia becomes, the hands that…raise.*

Faith supreme envelops.
Destiny, purpose in life develops.
The sights trouble

Children on the streets.
Aimless they wander, no tomorrow.

A place she must make.
Sense of belonging, she must create.
The home, the shelter.
Care for them, who has no other.

Protection from the elements.
Sun, rain, negativities super-abound
Bad influences, all around.

Excitement, awe, duty to fulfil.
Wondrous replicant, replacement.
Parent, downtrodden, indigent.

Orphans all, certainly not.
Require guidance.
Help, they need, predicament.

A new start make, for the children.
Venture, undertake…create.
Process 'not' simulate, concept different.
Revolutionary, to stimulate.

> *Bring about…change.*
> *Thus…have been made.*
> *The seed, long before.*
> *In the mind…laid.*

Chapter Nine

Dreams Create, Part Two

The Sister have played with the idea, what it would take to bring back together. What has been torn apart? For generations the people have been pitted against each other, they have been separated. For endearment to be rooted out, they have attempted. Nonetheless, shreds prevail, notions only, but could redress. What is was like, would be like?

For decency intact, remained.
Humanity, the bedrock.
Still entrenched, ingrained.
Lost not, the people retain.
Unbroken many, enough to sustain.

The concept, the general idea.
Togetherness...oneness.
The children require, they aspire.

The people would support.
The peace...the chance.
For peace...to teach.
The vow she makes.

She would keep.

The core message, the chances.
Sell she would, the idea.
What it would mean, the advances.

Towards, reconciliation.
Community participation.
Make the child, raise they must.
Instil that measure.
With confidence, entrust.

In their hands, place tools.
Peace Build
Resolution, Prevention, Inclusion.
Norms of Equality and Social Justice.

Conflict erase.
Acts bring about distrust, hate.
…Replace.

Violence unlearn…Unheard?
Violence disengage…Dissuade.

Possibility, kindness, towards each other.
Through…'peace education'…none other.

Not in a bubble, would sit.
The school system retained.
Public…private.
Taught…disseminate.

The message, lessons
Instructions on peace, nonviolence.
Takes place, mornings, evenings, weekends.

Every opportunity, not missed.
The virtues of peace, inculcated.
The Sister would insist, all participated.

The Immaculate One, Home.
Named after the child.
They all aspire to be.

> *Innocent...unsullied...unstained...un-stymied.*
> *Victims not...but masters...their destiny.*
> *Pave the way...the torch they bear, carry.*

Hope, for the new generation.
The past, they cannot rely.
Move on, but not deny.

History, recollections of victimisation.
Can cloud the mind.
Thoughts, judgement, imagination.

However, it will guide.
Shape, help fulfil their destiny.
What...Not...to be.

But one, of anew.
Of consideration, generosity.
Never again, animosity.

Towards each other, what has been broken...rebuild.
The lost desire, hope cradle...reanimate.
Mutual destiny foster...revivify...resuscitate.

The people who have supported the Sister, all involved will not be disappointed. What they have managed to achieve. In the short space of time it did take, their eyes could not believe. Behavioural changes on display, bonds being made, brothers, sisters found, promising results. An atmosphere conducive, for the intentions it was created. The sense of security, family life, chance to play ...study

Would greet, Patrice, Marcel, Dalia, the homecoming finally, would assume roles immediately. For health checked, physical, special needs and mobility, importantly, mental competency. The three would pass, Patrice however, excelled surpassed. His intellectual acuity intact, were not diminished, by the years spent, not in school, but in hardship.

Cap the driver, the giver.
The source of inspiration.
Encouragement and mentorship.

Read what I read, he would insist, would read for Patrice. Words cannot spell, put together, will learn later, he says. Squeeze out the knowledge, all the books that give. Inaccuracies in all, you will figure out, never now, always in time. Be brave, strong, temptation resist...think like the crowd. Never believe everything you read, are told. You will figure out, as they unfold.

The force becomes, unstoppable. In his mind...drawn, armed and ready to take on the world. Patrice will encounter many obstacles, but persevere he would, through the challenges.

115

The years that follows, the quest for higher education. Demoralised at times, confronted by what seems impossible. The task, the burden Patrice bears, to set an example, for his brother and sister to follow. Excellent reports, the reckoning of sorts, the protégé, leader in the making.

Results that bear his name 'Patrice Lumumba Losaka'... 'thanks for the heir'. He was named after the most famous Tetela, he came to earth on the eve of the leader's birth. Noble, his mother would give to him the greatest gift. The name that would carry him through thick and thin. But hoped, he would not succumb, to the same fate that, that followed him.

Born into poverty.
The 'Abyss'.
His destiny awaits.
One, Noble thinks of greatness.

First look, she saw in him, underdeveloped and tiny. But, the look in his eyes, hunger and surprise, his mindset strong, resolute he did not cry. In his mother's hands, accepted his fate, his future...await. Gone, but always in another's hand. His fate they carried, he...retained.

For the many problems.
Patrice have encountered.
From the moment of birth.
A life uncertain, hell on earth.

Hunger at all times, problems around every bend.
He never knew another, what life 'could' be like.
Or, how it will end.

But knew he wanted better.
The chance, an opportunity, is all it would take.
The question to answer.

The 'gift' he carries.
Call it a spark, flame.
Endure it would.
Precarious uncertainties.
Could never, dampen, tame.

Fed the drive, desire deep inside.
His character, inherent, developed, displayed.
Stand apart, did not capitulate.
Surrender to the forces negative, resistant to change.
Expect the worst, see in others, they would.

Absent, sense of reasoning.
The fundamental cause.
Understanding circumstances.

They created, children inherited.
Blame them, problems they encounter
Inadvertently keep alive, perpetuate.
Solutions could not deliver, rest on their shoulder.

State of the country, significance impair.
Encumber prosperity
Engender not, upward mobility.
But disability, leading to despair.
Burdensome, worry, future unclear.

What do they expect, poverty, conflict.
Years of destruction, vengeance.
Retribution, they inflict.

They lack the will.
Sense of responsibility, denied.
Drawback, the setback, they relied.

Placed in their hands, his formative years, Patrice understands.
What is expected, as he was told! Cap, his father envisioned
for him. The endless evenings, lengthy discourses, lessons on
greed, violence, conflict. Sister Beatrix, from where Cap left
off, would pick up the 'baton' speak for teaching, learning…
motivation.

Peace he learns, continue momentum, conception.
Mastery to follow, realisation, appreciation. Just part of the
proposition, Patrice's…education. More to go, university,
research, training…political acumen. All part of the plan, the
programme falls into place.

The hurdles he realise would never dissipate. The quest,
the journey for one's destiny…complete. The penultimate
stage, for university Patrice would prepare. He would muster
the courage, what is needed, qualifications he must attain for
acceptance, examination…entrance. The Sister, his biggest
supporter, cajoler…propagator.

The 'hope' that lies in the few.
The people would depend.
The change to bring about, recompense?

The sins of the father…the generation disarray befall.
The past they must confront.
Steady they go…unravel.
Complexities…originations of conflict.
Problems…weaved.
Synthesising realities on the ground.
Resulting difficulties…compound.

…Cap, now that the children has settled, begins with his business venture. Only with his trusted friend and brother, Leo now his partner. A transport company, informal however, will fill the niche created by the mining related sector. The need they saw, fortunes not to be made, but nevertheless, legitimate. Enough to maintain a comfortable existence, help them to settle down, as they are going in age, not the opposite. They rented a small house, premises to live in, with an office to conduct the business. They started with a single medium sized truck, within a year add another. By the year following would add another. They would recruit drivers and loaders as the business expanded. Service the many shops, construction, trading, and restaurants. Booming to say the least, but busy enough their feet.

An informal economy, they need not register or pay any taxes. One of the many causes that hinders development, does not advance it. Wealth remains, in the few hands they are exchanged. The purse, the coffers, only in the end, it is the state and the people that suffers. The system, the structure for taxation is not in place. Prosperity for some is guaranteed, wealth they do not share, never mind the people's need. The benefits accrue, for Cap, small and medium enterprises, large ones too. The state the problem, the leaders who lack the foresight, courage to engage the situation. Not take from the rich, give to the poor. But only a form of equitable distribution, for their livelihoods to ensure.

In many countries this exists, the problem of taxation persists. The nexus with poverty, development, health, education and the rich. Cause of disparity, in the many developing countries. Cap, and, those of his ilk benefits largely, they do not see the problem, and are blind to reality. Lost is that sense of responsibility.

Splendid goes, their dreams are coming through, finally, financial security. Cap and Leo have reached, their hard work has paid off. Gamble they did, their lives on the line, many a time. In darkness existed, the years of conflict, mining, they have made it.

Come unscathed, tortuous lessons, their future shaped.
Never again would think, go back to that time.
Unpredictability, uncertainty decline.
The state, the conditions of civil war.
Inhuman existence, human extinction
The mind, discombobulation.

Cap, vengeance eats him away, tears him inside.
Put an end to this mess, in Leo confide.
Makes no sense, dissuade in vain.
Leo attempts, but, fresh the pain.
Joseph's betrayal, in his mind, must indemnify.

Leo will continue to look after their affairs, the business. And the children entrusted with Sister, looked after very well. Cap, the short break he takes, he calls a spell. The Kivus return, the place for retribution, he knows too well. His connection guarantees, the resources and the men he needs. Hunt down and put an end to Joseph, once, and for all. Annihilate his memory, the legacy must decimate, for his murderous contempt. He would make with haste, with urgency and a one track mind. If he dies, it will not be in vain. He has done more in life, than could any man dream. To the children, he has not said goodbye, they will understand, if he should die. Their future he has created and secured, his legacy he believes, is intact.

In the Kivus would find something different, from that he left behind. Groups splintered, unrecognisable formations, and associations. See the faces of his men, the few have survived. Their appetite for death, has since long gone, they have seen too much, have borne. The inducement is not enough, for that type of life to go back. They are happy though, the joy that their Captain have survived.

The years of conflict, the terrain, the communication disconnected. 'The reality is different, they insist, the grudge he bears, they must make him forget it'. Take him to a grave unmarked, not a monument or shrine. Nondescript, on the small plank of board emerges. From what used to be a mound of earth, 'R I P' not any words. Here is your friend, dead he lies, Cap did not say, but he believes, they may have falsified.

Sinister, Joseph met the maker, rather, his life's taker, the Colonel. The one too many gambles, they explained, the scheming too much to handle. Cap discovers, ended his life, dazed, taken aback, an overwhelming sense of remorse covers him. He loved his friend, they have been through so much together, a sad way to end. How he would have confronted him, what would have been said? Would he have done as the Colonel did, just shoot him in the head?

It felt worse than if he had done it himself. The years that passed, sleepless nights. The vengeance that drove him, what consumed his thoughts. While his enemy 'the one' lay in the ground, long gone. Life is funny, he thinks, hindsight reason brings. What seems important, is sometimes irrelevant.

This is the end, closed, this chapter of life,

His family long gone, now his friend.

What remains, the family and the new life he has built.

Now return, carry only memories, no longer guilt.

See in them, what could have been.

If his family had the chance.

But, the triangulation.

Conflict, greed, and circumstance.

Wiped, away.

Back to life, this present day.

Chapter Ten
Politics, Then

Phase One

The Democratic Republic of the Congo. The political conditions that exist, and the realities on the ground. Has been shaped by 'decades' of political mismanagement, patronage, and military escapades. Every mistake made, everything 'not' to do, done it. Mobuto's daring, from the birth of the nation, would trigger the avalanche of chaos, political turmoil, and levelling. The ideology, counter intuitive, instituted to bring down, rather than build.

Regional, national, and international. So many interests, and divisions, boggles the mind, all lacking in consensus. It created disadvantages and tensions. Pre-independence movements, local leaders added to the problem. Grip on power Mobuto ensures, makes mandatory 'Popular Movement for the Revolution' membership, every citizen endures. Cemented grip on power, fosters in mind, the figment, he is the nation's father.

Name, of country changes, the relic stays the same, colonial styled repression, and favouritism reappears. State sectors not diversify, on rents depend, mining intensify. Decentralisation, political involvement, causal components, mystify.

The dictator's dream
Everything to suppress.
Democratic process, throws between.

Unmeritorious stratagem.
Chance and luck, friendship.
Loyalty, reign supreme.

The wedge, political elites dis-enfranchised.
Stand by, await opportunity, create instability.

Corruption, political malfeasance.
Becomes ingrained.
Forever...ever stained.
Politics in the Congo.
The model cannot throw off.
Kabila...to follow.

Mobuto no doubt.
Created the conditions.
All to scratch their heads, figure out.
The complexity, competition.
Militarism, warlordism.

Change, the transition one to the other.
Easy to make, the conditions dictate.

The stakes, high politics displaced.
Replaced, by the forces commanding.
Militias feuding and warlords descending.

The chance for constructive dialogue.
Stable political process and democracy.
Never to take off, advance.

A further militarised and political dispensation, would follow the defeat of Mobuto. Laurent Kabila would reverse the roles his predecessor once set up, promised. Triggering reprisals, a hailstorm of unrest, the political backlash for things not kept.

The stage was set.
The diffusion of power.
Military, rebels, politicians.
Ready to devour.

Political backstabbing.
Favour your own.
The blow, Mobuto dealt.
Kabila…returns.

Phase Two

As never seen.
Not fight with one or two.
But many, much more, between.

The power diversifies.
No longer in hands of elites.
Militia politics develops.
Control local authorities.
Villages, communities, chiefs.

Centralisation, once depend.
Decentralisation on them, descend.

Power, not in the hands of legitimate.
But the hands, those can grab it.
The idea, the notion.
If you can fight for power.
You deserve it.

Competency, not a requirement.
Brute force, shear will, what is pertinent.

The opportunity lost.
Leaders make every mistake.
Fecklessness generate.

In army officers, divest.
Political control, power, greed manifest.

Rebel movements, imitate.
Competition for resources, leaders create.

The many actors, players, the game politics.
Introduce the new concept
Military might, bullets the detriment.
Local authority, the target.

Superiority, exercise control
Under thumb, force rules.

Post-war peace, Kabila thought.
Would bring about settlement.

Too much power, retain.
The hands of the military, organised.
The rebels, Mai-Mai militia, disorganised.

Civil society, political parties, too much disdain.
Condescension, from hands take away.
What should have been promised, guaranteed.

Misunderstood, the role they play.
What could be possible?
Likelihood permissible?

Remain, military strongmen.
Within ranks, would purge.
Retain, strength, authority.
Threat of violence, the urge.

The 'militarisation' of politics.
Drives, economic competition.
Results, much advantage.
Types of alliances, sculpted.

Fast becomes, the new norm.
Leaders depend, not on electorate.
But disparate, conglomerate.
Armed, militaristic.

Tools of trade inherit, used to triangulate.
Power, greed, force, they need.
Cement discord, animosity.
Among state, community.

Political stability, they gambled.
What could have been, created?
Now…obliterated.

Thus resulted, the conditions.
For distrust among people.
The government.
Supporters, politicians.
Established, budding.
Armed groups existed.
The ones, fast becoming.

Every scene dominated.
Entanglement, duplicitation.
Violence engendered, manipulation.

This, the 'Second' phase of political distress.
Be it may, many not profess.
Colonisation, the period we must discount.

The overthrow of Lumumba.
Conditions created by Mobuto 'One'
The overthrow of Mobuto.
Conditions created by Kabila 'Two'

Post Second-War

This the 'Third' round.
Now political 'discontent'.
Adds another level.
Stress and resentment.

Generals, warlords, militia leader.
Removed from battlefields.
Placed in boardrooms.
Government's chamber.

Gives room to escalate.
Legitimise grievances.
Violence, bad behaviour.
Deeds rewarded.

All, they know now.
What to do, expected.
The standard, lower and lower.
The bar for government.

Spread, the theatre of conflict.
Parallel existence incorporated.
At the table, elites haggle over spoils.
On the field…violence…infused.
By ferocity…their blood…boils.

The chance come, change would bring.
The new dispensation, democracy?
Multi-party election, all they welcome.

Two thousand six, time not of joy.
Tainted by interference.
Dear leader, elites.
Retain magnificence.

Consolidate, grip on power.
Changes, more of the same.
Many predicted.

Armed groups refused.
To be integrated.
Led to clashes.

The 'Rally for Democracy'.
Would counter, the army inscripted.

Splintering, desertions, declarations.
Democracy, an aberration.

Impunity, violence.
Murder, rape, synonymous.
Would mar atmosphere.
Lead up to elections.

Democracy, built on conflict, never permitted.
Hands tied, are forced to give in, surrender.
Part of the process, Never.

Those, wrong have been committed.
Were never able, will never get justice.
From Rutshuru, mass graves remind.
Of a time, all ethnicity, defined.

> *Justice, and the 'Rule of Law'.*
> *Critical, for nation building.*
> *Democracy, only an undertaking.*

The general election, loom.
Atmosphere, uncertainty pervades.
In Eastern Congo, desperation, doom.

> *The Kivus…Congo sneezes.*
> *Cold…from which it catches.*

Kinshasa remain, heartbeat of power, retain.
Oversee brutality, quell concerns.
Discontent…forcefully.

Electoral discrepancy, delays.
The people protest.
Mow down with bullets.
What, whom they detest.

In Kinshasa, Goma.
Towns and villages.
Men, women, children, life disregard.
Death promote, did not protect.

In Katanga, same old rhetoric.

Crack down, arrest opposing activists.
Would be, the made up secessionists.

Human rights violations, certainly.
Crimes against humanity?
Cannot prove entirely.

Culmination, four decades, illegitimate rule.
What brings impunity, measure of force?
Violence... brutality.

Randomness, criminal acts sparse.
The events are separated.

The International Court.
Cannot connect, bring charges.
Identify, individual culprits.

Militia leaders, of war crimes accused.
Granted high positions in the army.
Leaves many bemused.

Payback, the many years of conflict.
Held the fort, government transitioning.
The one would become.
They would claim, retort.
Echelon unmatched, power wielding.
On them, must all now resort, depend.
The two thousand six elections.
Consolidates Kabila.
The younger one's grip on power.

The process continues unchanged.
Except for government's congealing, toughening.
Emboldened, gripped, consumed with force.
Commanded, militia equipped.
Undisciplined army, continue course.

Will proceed, the years go on.
Two thousand seven, eight, nine, ten fly by.
For he, that lives in wealth, power
Years not enough, the venture.

The people, each passing year.
Remember not a moment, chapter, spell.
Peace, good fortune, political stability.
Marked a time, their children to tell.
Periodisation, cadence, further decline.

> *Legitimisation…the right.*
> *Use of violence*
> *…Monopolisation.*
> *Violence…used.*
> *State…held.*
> *…Abused.*
> *…Designed.*

The elections that would settle scores, once and for all. Brought
only divisions, mud-slinging, recrimination.

The dictatorship of money.
Far from democracy.
The opposition rally.

Post-election confrontation.
Armed insurrection.
Coup d'état…fear.
Bemba pays tally.

Show who is boss.
Crush opposition militarily.
With sense of urgency.
Prepare, counter insurgency.

The elections did steal.
Hard pressed will keep.

Continue tradition.
Create the conditions.
Crush, recalcitrance.

They battle on the main boulevard.
The seat of power, Kinshasa.
Restore, democracy, order.
With the use of rockets.
Tanks and mortar.

Cause, he fled.
Prisoners, summarily executed.
None will know, see.
What it is like, true democracy.

Every course of event, twist and turn.
Shaped by violence.

Scores killed.
In schools, children trapped.
Lessons, they learn.
In politics, how to get back.

Relative calm, year did elapse.
Did not prevent.
Harassment and intimidation.
Opposition they circumvent.

Historic…indeed.
The elections that changed nothing.
Fourty years…in the making.

Chapter Eleven
Politics, Now

The Congo, it would seem now destined, head down the path of eventual ruin. Every decision made, and every course of action, brings negative reactions. The consequence, of the use of force and violence. In the East, two years after the elections 'Peace'. Government forces, and rebels, resume full blown conflict. In the West, mame, kill, or arrest, those who protest.

Warring factions, immune.
Prepared for battle.
What it entails, often assume.
March on, blaze…trails.

In dire circumstance, people live.
Upheaval, displacement.
Fled homes in droves.
The driven, embattlement.

The Kivus, unenviable.
Over a million displaced
Unmatched, incontrovertible.

Every confrontation, skirmish.
Causes further destruction, damage.
To lives, property, life.
The process undignified.

The democratic process entailed.
Rule of law, equity and justice.
To build, deconstruct.
Absolute impunity, follows.
Many thought, a new construct.

Thoughts ingrained.
Bury that, which remains.
Hope for the future, they aspired.
Mourn the loss, the people.
Now the process, expired.

Demoralised, filled with shame, rage.
What could cause, such disadvantage?
The question for the century, wonder.
The time they had to ponder.

Every country has found its place.
The source of their content.
Stand out we still, on this continent.

The source of problems, many knows.
The few that matters, ambivalent.

It all comes, redounds overwhelmingly.
The juxtaposition.

Required political stability.
Proffered instability.

The foresight, imagination leaders lack.
The conditions that continue.
What is further created?
By holding on to power.
Despite setback.

Deny new dispensation.
Decentralisation, regional autonomy.
Federalism, the schism.
Based on facts, pragmatism.

But greed, power they need.
Continue to drive politic…King.
Maintain status quo, at any cost.
Millions of lives lost.

Lines on paper, drawn
Years ago, miles away.
Fuels conflict, to this day.

The deaths, thousand a day.
Brought by hunger, disease, violence
To none, anymore, dismay.

Distress, suffering, pain, desensitised.
What they would come to expect.
Now, realised.

The State…any given time.
Pre-post-war, the people could not rely.
Challenges made harder.
By the chaotic, destructive.
Divisive atmosphere.

The Revolution

Non-state, unarmed actors.
NGOs stand accused, instigate.
Civilian movements, initiate.
Politicise, weaponise, social activism.

Opposition must come.
In one form, some fashion.
Political parties stifled, submerged.
Militancy, revolutionaries, emerged.

The new, threat.
On government, does not relent.
Diverse, difficult to pin down.
Label, subversive element.

Attack and arrest.
Placed on trumped-up charges.
Free speech restrict.
Reserved for government.

Machinery derives.
The discourse, only one.
Regime's eyes.

The movement, ideological stance.
Generated by the people.
Champion, proponent, not 'one'.
Difficult to douse.
Bring down, put out.

Devised, comes up a plan.
To counter revolution.
Co-opt journalists, the new militia.
Fight with pens, no machine gun, bullets.
Spread false propaganda.

Persecute, those not on board.
Prosecute, for sowing discord.
Fill cells, jails, those who rebel.
Mutinous rivalry.
Kill the brave, chivalry.

Abhorrent, state sanctioned.
Murder journalists.
Those who fight for justice.

> *Create…atmosphere.*
> *…Conditions.*
> *Anxiety…fear.*

Shut down television, radio stations
All that questions.
State control, all that matters.
Theft, corruption, anyone mentions.

Risks limb, life, lost behind bars.
Freedom, justice, rights
Never again, realise.

The complex series of detention facilities.
Layers of bureaucracy.
Conceals agencies, responsibilities.

Mobuto era designed.
Now far more notorious.
Than what he had in mind.

Courage that drives the man.
Sacrifice freedom, and their life risk.
For them, mere circumstances.
The pursuit, change conditions now.
For them and for future generations.

The political conditions.
Conducive to stability, development.
And, good governance.

To live in freedom, free from fear.
Fundamental for human security, fulfilment.
Critical, in pursuit of one's.
Livelihood, occupation.

> *Noble, the cause they fight.*
> *Die in process, they might.*
> *Martyrs become, heroes their name.*
> *Will live on, struggle sustain.*

Fought, died.
For independence, they did.
Fight goes on, dictatorship.

Tyrannically, engorged.
Shambles resulted.
Inevitably, forged.

Strong, political leadership required.
Institute, bring about changes.
Assume role, responsibility, control.
Difficult without mandate.

Division, fragmentation.
Ensures non-compliance.
Damn their state, their law.
To their people, violence.

> *The rule of law and justice*
> *Inextricably tied to politics.*
> *The climate, the circumstances.*
> *Degradation…trepidation.*
> *From the top down.*
> *Permeates every level.*
> *Debased…immoral…detestation.*

The best chance, four decades evades.
To escape clutches, violence and conflict.
The chance missed.
Focus on people and business.

Development and education
Health of the nation.
Squandered, lost, missed opportunity.
Never return, augury.

The chance, set the standard.
New things to come.
Politics, government.
Abandoned.

Confident, should have been.
Instil in mind, transcend.
Divisive politics, echoes past.
In war, hatred, remained trapped.

Rely instead, donors, foreigners.
The community recognised.
They in us see, the need, the urgency.
The future, possibility.

We are not defined.
Conditions, they gave us.
Our bad luck, their design.
Shame on them.
All…decline.

Our saviours, comes in vests.
Khaki, fluorescent.
Certainly not our government.
Surely, to our detriment.

To such an extent.
We need outside involvement.
Introduce concepts, political process, rights.
What should be expected, relevant, required.

In light of what exist.
Conditioning, the downward march.
Spiralling, deteriorating.

Violating every precept, notion.
Human right, injunction.
Structure, not in place.
Promised, committed, hesitantly.
Mannered diffidently.
People curtailed.

Affects, political undertaking,
Rights, redress.
Control maintained.

Take turns, rebels and militia.
Army, police, security forces.
Continue spate of abuses.

Power unmatched, government, civil authority.
Power vested, shrouded.
Unable, unchallengeable, unstoppable.
Unloose on the vulnerable.
The hungry, unpaid forces, corruptible.

Denigrating, masquerading.

Looting, robbing.
Violence perpetrating.

Sow fear, consternation, disgust, despair.
Stifle what remains.
Limited hope, freedom.
Ruination inevitably, create.

Unabate, integration.
Lead to force degeneration.
What dominates?

What was needed to maintain law and order? And, by all means, help in process for the country to recover. Instil that measure of trust and confidence. Support the government, the new constitution and build consensus. Instead, undoubtedly were misled. They would choose false peace, over the process. Damn the truth, as the forces compel. They instead recruited, incorporated those who committed human rights abuses. Not exempt from crimes against humanity. The new law they would greet, bypassing immediately.

Outmanoeuvre justice.
The political reform evaporated.
All part, would be apportioning.
Geared towards equality.
Peace and justice.

They are one and the same.
It flows from each other.
The concepts they were misinterpreting.

Not a simple undertaking,
Understanding, politics in the Congo.
The complexity, scale, breathtaking.

A dilemma.
Understanding, the depth.
This quagmire.

Much more than could, anyone bargain.
It is a disservice to try capture.
All that's been done.
Continues to happen in the Basin.
In a chapter, book, even volumes.

A nation, born in conflict.
Every era, political gesture.
Shaped by it.
Goes with each other.

Hard to let go, throw off.
The yoke of violence.
Repression, political interference.
Destruction.

The enormity, understanding challenges.
Faced by citizens.

Remised, if not mentioned, details.
Slightest, that changes trajectory.
Political direction, confrontation.
The future of the people.

Ambition, aspiration, sacrificial devotion.

Confronted, by problems.
Their many, disadvantages.

Unable to respond.
Adds to their frustration.

Resistance...struggle...bred into people.

All they know, bow to pressure.
Conform, up, they measure.

Conditions inherited, further created.
The round that takes, never gives.

Your life, your future.
Your dreams, perished.
Conflicts, abounded.
Conflicted, astounded.

Much have been written...talked about.
Not a shroud of mystery.
But a cloud...dominance...mastery.

Each time relate.
Rehash history.
Brings up hate.

Less talk, more action.
Deal with complexity.

Find solutions, bold new.
Confront, situation.
Challenge, administration.

> *Been going on too long.*
> *Put an end.*
> *The people…future…depend.*

> *To the violators.*
> *Elites…political…leaders.*
> *…Comeuppance.*

Chapter Twelve

Emergence, Part One

Patrice now only seventeen, manages again to achieve something really extraordinary. At that age, one only can dream. October fourth, two thousand ten, he enters The University of Lubumbashi. The seat of learning, but dissenting, opposing authority, autocracy and dictating superiority. They have challenged before, but the cost tremendous they endured, death, injury, brutal crackdown. The movement was torn open. Crushed, massacred, horrendous they were murdered. Children not adult, commando forces by order garrot. Tame at any cost, opposition, agitation and confrontation.

Mobuto, would put out the spark they have been promoting, building and instilling. Giving voice to opposition movements, they were all challenging. His absolute rule, the monarch in the making. The king of Zaire try to bring down, well much deserved ire. Much more than expected, what impacted, general consensus, the feeling, community at large, he then relented.

He was forced, he gave in then reform promised. Would have the last laugh though, so cunning, will avenge with retaliatory undertaking. Of all the dark times, moments, that marked the rule of Mobuto. Would be the one, most brazen, brutal, cruel and vicious. Designed to instil fear, crush hopes, dreams and create despair. It started in eighty nine, but would culminate in a brutal act the year following. Rage filled with hate, sadistic beyond measure. The crackdown on innocent student protesters.

In solidarity with their fellow students.
Organised a vigil, sit in, march, protesting.
Dire conditions faced by students, general public.
For the corruption, greed, accounted for disease.

Met instead, not by discourse, understanding.
But by force, crack of whip, slicing, muzzling.
Would bring under, dissent, opinion.
The two headed monster.

Student movements, leaders in making.
What they should engender, by use force render.
Dissolved, washed away, non-evolved, banished.
Create climate of obedience, subservience.
Hundreds murdered, arrested, dejected.
Professors who criticise, exiled, detained, vanished.

Pained, crackdown on students, too much, sustain.
Ally traditional, new one, wave goodbye.
Will continue state, spate of repression.
Intimidation of opposition.
Unions, women civil, student movements.
Lay the foundations, things to come.
The decade to follow, war, political turmoil.
Exclusion, repulsion.

Never to be part of system.

Patrice continues down the path of perpetual learning. Ever increasing his knowledge, gaining understanding. Enrols for courses in politics, history and philosophy. A bachelor of science will be, the icing on the cake, showcasing splendid ability. Prove he is the best, whatever he sets his mind to be. At any cost, opportunity not lost, will prove to all, finally.

He feels as if he was born for this, politics and philosophy comes to him naturally. His lecturers all supportive, young, bright, most foreign trained. Gets world perspective, no longer in mind contained. He looks at himself 'differently' his people and country. The realisation dawns, all he has been told by Cap and Sister Beatrix, now presently. Comes together, it makes perfect sense.

He remembers what Cap told him.
About believing everything.
They will make their case.

Me, I will mine.
Form my own opinion.
Judgement pass, I will decline.

Would it help our conditions?
Change situation, blame constantly.
Those who have mistakenly.
Made wrong decisions.
Chosen unwisely.

Politics, from historical perspective.

Could be dissected, retrospective.
Gives consideration.
Hindsight the luxury afforded.

What could have?
Should have, been done?
When decisions confront.

Weak men, influenced easily.
Not shoulder blame.
But shares responsibility.

Trailblazers not.
The men who charted course, created history.
Great, but greater by themselves.
Answer to none, but to historicity.
Of greatness, even mediocrity.

Napoleon Waterloo
Thousands their cemetery, despised.
But, aggrandised, memorialised.

Patrice empties his mind.
No preconceived notion.
Pronouncement reserved.
For those that have served.

Posthumously recalled.
Instances that merit.
Admiration, enthralled.

Freedom fighters.
Fought for Africa's independence.
All great men, could have been.
Greatness only, some retain.

Mugabe…celebrate 'no' longer.
Nkrumah…we will 'always' remember.
Dead men can do no wrong.
Wait until they are gone.
Plays in his head, repeatedly.

Everyone is nice to Patrice, fellow classmates, and lecturers. The students represent almost every tribe found in the Congo, but there is no animosity amongst them, as seen in the outside world.

There is this bond, a sense of dependence formed between each. A common objective, willingness to help, carry each other, teach. Learn from one another, create friendships, out they reach.

As they search, find their purpose, make sense of what they learn. To the real world apply, for many concern. A job, a future, a place in the world. For the thousands that turn out, there is no return.

Questions oneself, why study, why suffer, why live in debt? All this for a future, doors shut, luckless and dependent. Look around, thousands of children on the street. The alternative to being educated, life dire circumstances greet.

Considered fortunate, above all stand, the university graduate. On them, much depend. The future of the country, governance and much needed development.

The very children, they are admired.

For many years The Congo stood, forever it seems, its nationhood. At the bottom of the table, children's rights and infant mortality. The sliding scale dismally represent, the lack of concern and irrelevance. Children viewed as impediments, good only as child soldiers, beggars and house keepers.

Look up they see, at the university.
What could possibly represent.
The chance, the hope.
The future benevolence.

Pure in mind, untainted by greed, division.
Leaders in the making.
Mind, thoughts clean, create vision.

Place, country should be.
Their roles, responsibility.

Create conditions for the protection.
Betterment, advancement of children.
What they believe, increasingly.
Lies with them, on shoulder rests.
The children, their future, best interests.

Children's concerns, disregarded.
Forever in this case.
As conflict, politics, takes centre stage.

Too much to do, so much to repair.
Resources too little, mind never despair.

The smallest, weakest, hands cannot reach.
Meek, needs advocates.
Before it is too late, fall through the crack.
To fabric of society, never get back.

Despite beliefs, worldview of The Congo. All they think, seem to know, does not hold true unless in their shoe. People, all over the world, their aspirations, dreams of a better life unfold, their goals few, one or two.

In the Congo, manifold.
As conditions propel.
Dreams multiply, expand, excel.
Never for one instance believe.
The people, developing Congolese.
Dreams less than developed.
West, North, South, East.
Better life they seek.
Conflict, worry free.

Now understand better, further they see. That their future depend, begin and end with children. Create channels, avenues for improvement, foster in mind a sense of greatness. Dreams can be achieved through education and development.

Realising this, where he now stands, that place whence he looked. Patrice forms in his mind, the notion, an understanding of what they need. For development to succeed, they must have peace. Can one man make a difference? He would often ask himself, does not look too far…

…Mandela, South Africa.

Life sacrificed for peace, freedom.
For this, he shall strive.
Guided by history.
Circumstance shaped trajectory, contrive.

Too young, much to ponder.
Worry, weight on shoulder.
Feels his duty.
Callow not, missed opportunity.

Chance, a better life given.
Favour return, undertaken.

Doubt, eradicate.
Relevance, purpose, elucidate.
In mind would stimulate.
Thoughts of freedom, justice, equality.
Long ago, would only speculate.

Feel, taste, on the cusp of something great.
Extricate, liberate, senses possibility.
Dreams can be achieved, higher probability.

Feelings of urgency.
But not desperate militancy.
Birds, feather.
Thoughts, plan action.
They pulled together.

As the semester closes, first year.
Atmosphere, thick the air.

Two thousand eleven, election season.

There is Trepidation, smell of fear.
The time disregard, season.
Inhibitions thrown out, for problems prepare.
Would, should they involve themselves.
As they compare.

Time ago, memory not long past.
Historically, presently, wanton brutality.
Those stand up, put down mercilessly.
Chance?

Patrice feels something deep, tearing inside.
Have not yet realised.
But feelings cannot hide.
Attitude towards authority.
Disgust, mistrust mostly.

His yearning, revolutionary spirit.
This rebellious native.
Unguided, pathfinding.
Difficulty conforming.
Needs tempering.

Believes, he knows everything.
Not alone, but lonely.
If they could only.
No one understands.
How it feels, what it means.
The burdens carry.

The dreams many.

Blames authority, created dependency.
Climate uncertainty, never opportunity.
Suffering likely.
With disregard.
They look upon.
Reason, we now shun.

Should have seen, never keen.
Known better, years all suffer.
Perpetuate, climate of hate engender.
Debilitate, from poverty lift, slender.

Misguided, swell-headed, hatred.
Dumbfounded, astonished.
Sensibility rejected.

Patrice feels shame.
No community.
Sense of belonging.
Despite, respite, offering.
New friends showering kindness.
Welcoming, the home creating.
Family, generosity follows him.
Destiny dictating.

He blames the state.
Leaders, all failing.
Suffering, desperation, evident.
Greed, corruption, malevolence.

Results, they envisioned.
Concerned?
Not their problem.

As motives dictate.
Condition create.
Generations, development.
Education denied.
Poverty stricken.
On strangers' kindness relied.

Denial, dependency.
Incoherence displayed.
Change unlikely.
Eyes open see.
Tide brings change.
Possibility?

Chapter Thirteen
Emergence, Part Two

What would be the best course of action? On what will they decide? Go down the road others did? Or, for them by time would abide? They know it is a gamble they must take, there is no room for compromise. Other, than protest, then what is it? If they go down this road, what would they achieve, when no one did? Highlight their views and make proposals, the changes what they see is needed. The Challenges that confront, and the problems faced with the education system. Social issues they will ignore, this was raised once before. But obedience was costly, and violently restored.

The chance must snatch, they would grasp.

Elections would bring the opportunity. At no other time does he care, the politicians all want something, will prove who dares. When the iron heats, one must pound, in order to mould. Shape the discourse, drive the message home. Patrice will encounter, a sense of daring like none other.

They will take, they will seize the moment, squander not one second. Fiery all, hungry for change, would go alone, or align with campaign. Wary, caution not throw out the window, plan, focus on strategy. Reduce the cost of tuition, if not, then the question of subsidy. Not unfair, not one nerve they would touch, strain on treasury likely not. They should support the issues raised, the help needing, respond they would to the pleading?

> The mark of a caring government.
> Focus, attention placed on children.
> Development, education.
> Signs, a first class.
> Second, third world.
> Matters not, the nation.

It is advancement in whatever form, or shape it takes?

Above all, opportunity, thence it creates. Commend we must, the nations, above all place children. Despite restrictions, poverty induced pressures and problems. In them invest education, the future in everyone's interest.

Education should be free, not inhibiting or prohibiting. Cost effective and unrestricting, children willingly learning.

Dominating the agenda on which they bargain. A sense of reason and clear voice, fair minded, never treason, us? Patrice and the others, would use this strategy unrelentingly. Adopt an attitude, the plan, non-confrontational, designed. Illicit response, not force, brutality, as they would often see. A different approach they would use, from government, would gain sympathy, from the people, empathy.

The students, the movement does not want much. Less stress on parents, reduced costs, not free lunch. They have their share, politics heats up, heads get hot. They must maintain control any cost, would be disastrous, if lost. Patrice would have his way, influence the strategy, the gambit non-violence, seeking fairness and mercy. Cannot fight the state, all have tried but they failed. The movements, armed groups, and some states.

> *Ghandi, King, Mandela.*
> *Fight they did.*
> *Brought down empires.*
> *Not one bullet fires.*

They too shall prevail, with good sense and reason, align with the right person. People who want to make a difference, using non-violence, the other coercive influence.

> *Challenge, not malign, damage.*
> *Good relations, could only bring about.*
> *Not by burnt bridge, manage.*

As they vie for leadership and control, some beat chest, trying to impress. Senior year threes, repeaters, even the beginners. Patrice observes and listens attentively. As often notices, they stray foolishly, strategies displayed incomprehensibly. The topics, the points too much, their agenda too heavy, they lose touch, they are without finality. Patrice the natural leader he is, listens, learns and speaks last.

Will first, set agenda, if asked.
Discipline, Cap taught him.
Observe everything.
React strongly to nothing.

Expose not yourself.
Thoughts, mind.

Unless to impress.
But only in time, need arise.
Otherwise, useless.

Conditions dictate.
Opportunity create.
Weighed carefully.
In mind decide.
The benefits, one, all.
Yourself, then choose
Aim high.

Then would come: 'what do you think Patrice' the most senior
would ask. That, which resonates, the words comprehend, the
question well read. For not one second did he think about.
The words from his mouth comes out. The thousand times has
gone through his head.

'A different approach is what we need'.

Coming from a boy, a young man not even eighteen. All
they listen, what they do now stop. Await, the other shoe to
drop.

Do we learn from the past?
Said rhetorically, not question asked.

We all see what happens.
All riled up, confront, challenge.
We are put down with force.
Violently crushed.

We retreat, tame.

Never to show again.
Contempt, disobedience.
In us rests, blame.

It is what they want.
Be like them, depend.
Violence induced.
Violence beget.
The cycle flows, no end.

A peaceful approach, never try.
Maturity, civility, the law.
We should instead, rely.

Many choices avenues.
Ways to advance causes.
Violence, instead chooses.

Block roads, bridges.
Burn tyres, down buildings.
Destroy shops, beat their supporters.
Shocked, did not get what we want.

…Well said, were they listening?

An awe, the prodigy, on him have been waiting. Who knew they needed, if so, now impressed. The gift horse not look, his mouth spells out, his advice they took. With caution, they would press, onward through the many challenges, and obstacles that lies ahead. Confronting what it seems, impediments and predicament thrown. In their way, their face, to crush their hopes and dreams. So many excuses, they come up with, when they try to advance, reasons for never, backward instead, forever.

Patrice, of age becomes, he has emerged so conditioned. His training, the endless nights, the lessons, his dreaming. Never 'any' sense of belonging he was searching. Now finding his calling, his purpose, his place, the people surround him.

Expectations fill.
Self-worth-image-esteem glistening.
But, only the beginning.

Trials, failures, must come up.
Prepare to lose, but give best shot.
Take in stride, drawback loss.
But success, smallest, with pride.

Conditions difficult, extract.
Pessimistically, not.
Pragmatically, on track.

Optimism, the brain affect, expecting.
Encouraging behaviour, beguiling.

Disregarding deterrent.
Yourself, set-up.
Movement, set-back.

Irreversible, will be.
Jumping in, blindly.
Mistake made, times many.

Analytically, strategically.
Coordinate, devise, plan.
Your fall-back position.
The thought enhance.
Not one, but many.
Each member advance.
Expand the pie.
From greater will choose.
Brainstorm a must.
Then troubleshoot.

Prepare for unexpected.
What if? They sit and listen.
Or beat, fire bullets, theorise.

The succession plan.
Strategy, leadership.
Come up with, if can.

In ignorance, believe.
From people expect.
Surprise them we must.
Will gain respect.

For many years, the fool.
Violence instigate, the tool.

Would use, bring down, cripple.
The opposition, the movements.
The protesting people.

Student's view, opinion and voice.
Not one and the same.
Agenda different, purpose.

In one stroke they contain.
Broad, sweeping, covering.
Protestation, opposition, dissent.

Children's concern, student vent.
Not a threat, seek stable government.
They are in sense, dependent.
Stability that can only bring.
Conscientiousness, reasoning.
The sense of duty fulfil.
The environment, development needing.

Incitement leading violence.
Away change course.
Channel movement.

Centre of attention focus.
Resource rather spend.
Corruption, kickback.
Mischievous.

Trust this is what they seek.
'Trust' this is what 'we' seek, build.
Tarnish they will, countervail.

Carefully, thread lightly.
Choose path, not upset.

Numbers small, sustain cannot.
Losses, break-up, abuses.
The masses, strategically uses.

First Protest
They prepare for what lies ahead.
Political backlash, possible bloodshed.
The dream, centre stage.
Would walk alone, or others' hand take?

Patrice tries able.
The First day gather.
Voice would muster.
He knows gamble.
Is it too much?
Environment climate.
Politically hot, unstable.
Prepare for trouble.
Hold up your signs, chant, sing.
Respond not, voices threatening.
Not block roads, pedestrians crossing.
Smile, in peace we come.
Highlight grievance.
Using non-violence.

On deaf ear would fall.
Made the news though, that's all.
Not a broken bone, busted lip.
Strategy that worked, enough said.

Take a bow, Patrice my boy.

Much to be proud.
Walk, raise your head.

First test, emerge victorious.
Who knows, the future hold?
What favours the bold?
Handsome, intelligent, brave, courteous.
Make wave, doors for him open, glorious.

On laurels rest.
Not continue protest.
Tried, succeeded.
They have the advantage.
The blueprint, future success.

The weapon, non-violence.
Smile, taken seriously.
Civility on display.
The evolution, revolution.

The struggle.
Those could, never would.
Mount violent campaign.
Revolt or insurgency.

Call it what they willed.
The many generations.
The world, not succeed.
Tried but failed.

Some have taken it too far.

Cause, did not stipulate.
But rather speculate.

Fedayeen to obstructionists.
Mujahedeen to terrorists.
Revolutionaries to communists.

When does it stop?
Do they stick to the cause?
Does everything evolve?
Just because?

They all get lost.
Paved the road, hell.
Dreams, no goals.
Ambitions, no plans.
Wrong intentions, swell heads.

This shall not, peaceful warriors they are, befall them.

Violence have always used.
Has never worked.
What would it take?
Different approach?

Something right.
Something good.

What the world knows.
History taught, lessons not.
Violence, force.

Some capitulate, give up.
Lick wound, heals.

Comeback, vengeance, hate.
False peace cannot dictate.
Peace, cannot force.
Voluntary, helps right cause.

What the 'few' does not want.
Those who prosper, succeed.
Of those, that kill.
The poor, that suffer.

Resource prop-up.
The hands that feed.
The soldiers, people, fight, bleed.
For mouths so puffed.
Masticate cannot.
But ingest greed.

Their bellies can never fill.
The few with pride, instil.
Watch they fight.
Handout, people shout.

Cry, lookout, change comes…doubt?

Chapter Fourteen
The Struggle

Patrice is, in a sense guided, whether he is in mind, or his ancestor's looks upon. Or could be simply by observation, looking at the ill-advised misguided, others, those lacking direction. Make not the mistake, and again, and again. If you cannot fight the system, work around it, go through it, but never against it. It is a good thing they did, test not their fate reduce their chances, their goals to achieve. The forces would cut short, they make not the advances. Would be their worst fear, name on paper, the 'black.'

List put together.
State sum up, distribute.
Forces carry out, execute.
Intimidation, victimisation.
Sustained campaign.
Busted head, shots fired at.
Left for dead.

Damned, for standing up.
Demanding change.
Send the message.

Criminals, outcasts.
Considered terrorists.

Intervene at every level.
Political party, individual.
Even by standing.

Up to…hither.
From any year not different.
Not worst, nor better.
Who knows the measure?
Violence, brutality, torture.

Not stellar, two thousand eleven elections.
Nothing different, nothing to report.
No reason, except fallout.

Usual of course, disputed.
Reasons always, they refuted.
Contradicting, polarising.
Incumbent, opposition.
Independent candidates.

The spate of attacks.
The state of affairs.
Guided by history.
Brute force, dominance.
Claims of victory.
Emergency.
For vengeance prepare.
Violence the tool.

Ready, able to use.
Solve, could not otherwise.
Dispute.

Not even in homes safe.
Activist, opposition supporter.
Look, the part.
Play, the part.
Licks, if you gather.

Curfew, self-imposed exile.
Else, come for you, detain.
Might not see again.

Who knows what happens.
Behind closed doors.
Speak not bars, cells, walls.

Though carry.
The haunting memory.
Stains, blood spattered.

Lost hopes, dreams.
Lives snuffed out, screams.
The family remain, worry.

Their loved one.
Their hero gone, lost fight.
Asymmetrical though, it might.
Life put up, died.

Killed on the streets.
Bodies removed quickly, cheaply.
Back of truck, bus, no ambulance.
Forces, security, the Republicans.

Cover they would traces.
Hidden bodies, the fallen.
Different places.

Threaten, co-opt officials.
Cause of death, keep mysterious.
Bullets remove, hide evidence promptly.
Fool they must, all attempt, family.

> *Search high, low.*
> *Theirs, dear ones.*
> *For love could bestow.*
> *A proper send-off.*
> *All they can do, know.*
> *Befitting warrior, valiant.*
> *Died not, for nothing.*
> *But the cause.*
> *Martyr…defiant.*

Patrice and the others, the small band of sisters and brothers. Emerge unscathed, victorious, would fight again.

What could have been disastrous, their lucky stars count, fortuitous. Gives room, they gain momentum, prepare to take on greater challenge. Identify future leaders, would launch campaign, the 'Youths for Peace' the signal, the call, would send out to one and all.

Would all have voice?
As democracy dictate.
The freedom of choice.
Will put up nominate?
Those that stand.
Not sit at table, delegate plans.
But down in trench, dirty hands.
Toil sun, rain, against odds.
Even done in vain.

Who would they pick?
Who did they see?
They would select, he that stands out.
The highly intelligent, stocky year three.
Bosco the soft spoken, a natural born leader.
The son of a chief, happens to be

Nominated by year one.
Lillianne, shy, beautifully.

The sister, none can tell.
Figure out, try as hell.
Compare…
Soft velvet chocolate, subtly.
Against…
Dark roasted coffee, bodily.

Could not be more different, variant.
But their attachment, clear, apparent.
Can figure out, some would dare.
Their intelligence, drive.

Two of same kind.
Royalty it seems, superiority.
Naturally, of all dreams.

His right hand man choose.
To none surprise, could not dispute.
The place he has earned.
The cap he wears.
Head of strategy, research affairs.
The man who plans, everyone swears.

Now come, all depends.
Patrice would from front, lead.
New heights, thinking.
Planning, forecasting.
Rainy, sunny, day.
Boots on ground.
Blows, if they stay.

Move on, further away.
Find new audience.
Not city centre, parliament building.
What about bus terminus.
Highway, people passing.

Make their point, go slowly.
Attrition, eat away gnawingly.
One day would listen, well made.
Message delivered, inevitably.

Could not bypass, tried hard.

But, image they see.
Generation, replace identity?
Not contemporary, not long past.
Even recent memory.
But the future.
The new army, warrior.

The Youths for Peace.
Stand for change.
Collectively, individual rights, abundantly.
Settling, trickling, notwithstanding.
Violence reduction, leading cessation, termination.
Arbitrarily, summarily, extra-judicially.
The forces that carry out, merrily.

Halt! Come bring about change.
Would support, any individual, candidate.
Anyone sends clear message.
Tired of brutality.
Want free fair democracy.
Rule of law, equality and security.

Importantly, quality, stand up for, fight for.
But, must not hastily.
Be the change, show the change.
Example set, for all too see.

Most of all, seek.
End of impunity.
Collateral damage, the weak.
Those, cannot stand up.

Choices not made.
Though, believe subversive.
Support enemy, alternative.

The State of Affairs

The poor need, they suffer.
Government, opposition, squander.
Followers, supporters.
Live in squalor.

Nothing to eat.
Elites feed, get fat, and accumulate.
Wealth of live, conflict and abundance.
For nothing left, no inheritance.

Their families migrate.
Big cities, metropolis.
Home the master, colonist.
Now part, think become.
Looked, upon.
Disdain, distrust.

Matters not, loot fill.
Follow you will.
Our pattern instil.
Steal…bankrupt.
Displace…disrupt.
You can never be.

One of us.

In mansion, luxury, champagne.
To their people, misery.

Await, their turn.
If not, dead return.
The place, birth.
Travel on.
This place, earth.

Hallowed soil worship.
Die not for it.
Same one, abandoned, years gone.
Thought not, those behind, left rot.
Sacrificed coveted prize.
People paid price.
Land so precious, would die.
Better you, them.
Could multiply.

Must remain.
Carry on tradition.
Appearance…fight for change.
Replacement…
Duplicity…
Falsity…
Funny…strange.
People they fool…suffrage.

Corruption

One

Does not stop.
Not plan, build, enhance.
But drain treasury.
Central bank.
Congo certainly.
Many countries.
Developing, mostly.

Inclination, better.
Institution, stronger.
Indivisible, together.
Country greater, advanced?
Not chanced.
Not even, glanced.

Resonates, head.
Thoughts, frailty, fragility.
Created criminality.
The people, dependency.
The fraudulent conspiracy.

The vacuum made.
The goal, dictate.
The condition create.
Capture state.

No law apply.
Never laid, rely.
Loophole instruct.
Government, opposition.
Backer, financier, sameone.

Elites, class, top, none other.
Spoils gather.
Scraps throw.
Pitting, fight over.
Hierarchical order.
Sweet fruit they eat.

Bitter…seed.
People…devour.

All a game, well, they know.
Just as master would.
Now come to fore.

The new Leader.
Minister Prime.
Bestow paradigm.
Initiation competition.
Thievery enunciation.
Cleptocracy articulation.
Acquire, after fashioned.

All be damned.
Hell, what remains?
Dregs…nothing.
Loss…visceral.
Society…skeletal.
People…tatters.
Country…ruin.

Two

What, can you do?
Rebels, soldiers, rape.
Now leader, governor.
Plunder, State, eviscerate.
Nationalise, under.
Bring closer.
Asset strip.

Resource fall-off.
Somehow gather.
Find way, propagate, generate.
Wealth stimulate.
Desert barren, springs not.
Amplitude, multitude.

The lone traveller.
Quenches thirst.
Oasis, not first.
Many before, none after.
Extirpate, not rejuvenate.
Flood sense, desire.

Relocate vastness.
No one, nothing, abundant.
Not belong, longing.
Faced by one, all.
Those who acquire.
Find, no space.
Never, ebullient.

Though filled.

Ill-gotten, claim.
Wish, diminish.

Go back in time.
When exuberance.
When hunger.
Yearn, earn, alive.

Satisfy, gratify.
Friends, family.
Windfall share.
House, property.
Gifts splendidly, money.

All of the things that goes through his head, Patrice knows they cannot fix everything. But they can start somewhere, start with one thing that is, governing. Change the pattern of behaviour. People have done, they have tried, it has worked, now on this relied. The state of many countries, the resource they develop, in people trust. They did not squander, but invest in a good cause. In many countries, no resources, not even a drop. Yet the people and the country developed.

Kind and compassionate, leader in the making, he has all the right marking. Could one day become a minister, the people's representative, who knows, someday even the president.

He considers, remembers, the words of his father, what he uttered. Its importance and relevance, mark this day, acceptance.

Destiny, fate.
No man await, out run.
In time abide.
Never realise.
Hence, upon eyes.

The decades of pervasive misrule, they must centre on.
What could bring unity and stability? The unruly they must focus on, what could bring control, reliability and dependability. These disruptions many, to the cause, debilitatingly. Managing plurality, the challenges maturity supposedly manages.

Patrice have seen what could have been?
That vision, thought, imagination runout.
That age, wisdom and reason did not bring about
Now his youth, strength and tenacity comes out.
He must confront, he must stand up.
Face the fight head on.
Not take flight, but carry on.
Struggle for change.
At any cost.
Die if must.

The government kills civilian, but forgives rebellion.
Rebels fight, given life, continue to rape and plunder.
People fight for change, they die, now brought under.
The litany of abuse, nay, the weak confuse.
More than share, would rise one day.
Unable to take the suffering climate.
Disaster hell-bent, turmoil, belittlement.

Country after country, those govern.

Exclusively, precariously, prove unlikely.

Sustain grip, seams rip, threads shred.

Concrete, stone, gravel.

The people, cement.

Starts to unravel.

Break apart castle.

Bring down.

Kingdom fall.

Would build again.

Sure as day.

The Knight sustain.

King one, all, shape.

Destiny create.

Conditions anew…

…not manufacture, disaster, uncertainties.

Gamble the lives.

People no more.

Reveals the past.

On they go, fulfilled.

Joyful at last, rebuild.

Chapter Fifteen
He has Reached

Patrice is now in year three, and at the top of class as expected. He is beyond his years in intelligence and understanding. He is precocious, some might say, but not by those who understand him. They know it is not by fluke, nor is it by accident. The prescient one? Possibly, believably, would always as he does, see. The circumstances, the conditions, and the 'people' who are the 'creators'. What thought and imagination can only bring about, he has employed from day one.

Illuminate the hour, the sun would from above. Vision, the mind brightens all the time, hour, day, and lifetime. Patrice is never lost, he is seeing things clearer, and it is getting stronger, he is articulating better. Does not chance as others do, he would never court disaster. Foolishness with gamble, the others destiny and master.

He has started a part-time job, works evenings and on weekends, with his friend, the girl's brother. Soon full-time, Bosco promised, the result of the 'bond' that was created. Only by struggle and fight, some, revolution can unite. Sacrifice their lives many times, go down, and rise together as one.

Bosco, has moved on, it has been two years now. Will keep his promise made to Patrice, help him to run his family business. Land ownership, and acquisitions, and whatever it brings, rentals and leases, the squabbles, Bosco diffuses. They relied on, depend on, the mediator extraordinaire, his dispute settlement, beyond compare. The new Chief, the old one restful, retired, may soon sleep.

His sister, the shy beauty, in 'Patrice' has taken fancy. He pretends, his charade tough, the mask he wears, says stand-off. He can handle the difficulties, but not the pleasantries.

He is a born and bred warrior, he is a fighter, not yet the lover. She must tame, the beast within, his fighting spirit handle, in him ingrained.

In him borne.
Son of chief, not.
Soul that carries, result.
The mind create.
Extinguish doubt.
Made his thought.

He is tough, hard the shell, but a soft interior. Melt as she would often speak, he turns into butter. Sometimes would muster a few words responsive, ineligible, he confuses. She understands him, beckons response, Lillianne for Patrice, the beacon, trust. Always guided, he wonders, does he deserve this? Have done what? And is it enough? To instil confidence and trust.

He is not vain, his looks cannot.
Attitude it seems, what sustain.
Behaviour in error, tries to contain.

Reflection, introspection.
Appreciation given.

Show gratitude.
Means everything.
Need nothing.
Beyond reproach.
He that shows.

Sometimes we are unable, those who have past, and long gone, we make amends with those who carries on. What bothers? Our mind disrupt, our goals corrupt. We feel unfulfilled, we need to fulfil. The source that trouble, conciliate, intervene, never too late, not as it seem, propitiate.

Smooth as silk, Patrice goes.
Bent the mind that slows.

Corrupt, they cannot, Patrice, his brain, his mind brilliant.

He does not forget, but he figures out. The bewildering problems, he can handle anything. In boxes placed, the past, the future and the present he separates. What needs to be done? Things to come? Where he has reached? Where he came from?

He never forgets the people, and their faces. The circumstances that has shaped, and the conditions they have made. Holds the future, the key, the promises kept, to one and all, for himself meant, though not even said. He has formed, framed, he trims and prunes, controls and carries, and by expectations adjust. As Cap have said, leave for last, control or change, things he cannot.

Exasperates, those cannot figure out, infuriates, the fool. Cannot get a handle and grip, that which evades, the solutions and explanations. The doubts about, it runs amok. Befuddled, the weak and faint minded rejects, does not accept, reality flustered, Patrice has solved, licked.

Graduation Day

The sense of accomplishment, greatest some would say, it is graduation day. Patrice's name is called, he stands up, and walks to the front. The stage was set, welcome the graduants. He steps to podium, he does not look around, the prize Patrice focuses on. His bachelor's degree receives, Political Science, first class honours, much deserved congratulations.

He is beaming, but self-containing, he looks around, surveying. In the audience, smiling, cheering, all those who have guided and helped him. The way forward, they have nurtured, Cap of course most proud, stands up and shouts, that's my boy.

The crowd in front could not conceal his clearly, white teeth, it shines for all to see. Proudly, exuberantly, he cried happily. His arms wraps around Marcel, Dalia and Sister Beatrix, all now one. Patrice in his short life, have brought together, the glue that connects, all the parts, their life's thread.

In the days that succeed, when joy gave way. Reflects profoundly, what follows? Always does, Patrice. As the thoughtful among us always would. Where he came from, the hardships he has faced, the people by him stood and the lessons of life, engaged. Has now reached the point, the future that lies, figure out. The few thoughts finalise, not close off, things not done and said, round it goes, spins in his head. It confuses him not, must still work it out, as he thinks about.

Poignantly, Patrice reflects on his mother, not what he would have said, but she. Would have been so happy, a grown man now is he. Growing up as he did, the many challenges he faced. How he emerged, how he has gotten, now become.

Noble

One

What she might say.
No! Say would.

I am sorry my son.
I was not there for you, all along.
But, got you started.
I did, the race.
Long before I departed.

This earth, the created misery.
Pain, hunger, poverty, so much.
All around, inside me.

The things we cannot fight.
What takes our lives?

Confuses, places doubt about life.
How to carry on.
What it holds for us.

The struggle, pain one bears.
Turbulent at times.
Intense feelings.
Sense of despair.

Weaker can get, he that rejects.
Stronger can get, he that accepts.
Having said, ensure.
Remember one thing, never give up.
This is not, what life is about.

If you do there will be nothing.
Nothing that remains.
Our generation extinguished.
In time forgotten.

Fight you must.
Champion our name.
My legacy, kindness goodness.
In you now carry.

Your loss, your pain.
The hole, the soul.
Only you my child.
Your child, console.

Two

You are so precious my boy.
The being, the beautiful soul.
No one would understand.
The gift inside, you hold.

No one could ever see.
Only mother.
That is why, in you.
I have placed, me.

You did not see.
But felt me, must have.
My Spirit, your sense that guides.
My hunger, your drive, you strive.
For I caressed your face.
When you cried.

This the warmth you felt inside, was me.
You are the light.
My life, my love, it is what.

The stars, moon, light in the sky.
Guides you home, at nights you roam.
The sun that brightens your day, I am.

Held your hand, you stray.
When you were lost.
Brought you back.
The obstacle course.

Confuse you cannot.
Could some thought.
The good I did.
Brought you luck, sin did not.

Those who care for you.
All my doing.
Undone the gifts.
Those who need accepted.

Returns in your favour.
Kindness, the universe shall shower.
So shall it be, forever.

Dalia

Patrice was relieved to hear that Dalia has decided to stay on with the Sister. The Immaculate One needs all the help it can get, the Sister going down in age, accepts. She has expressed her wish to take her vows, not in marriage, but to her lord, to the church, her life will give. Serve the community, the people, and the children's needs, that quadruple. Carry on the work the Sister started, stand by her side all through out, till that day she succeeded.

She did not go on to university, in fact any education, tertiary. But her wit and intelligence would get her through any situation. Patrice was sure she would manage, better yet in safe place. Still at school, Marcel she will look after, the Sister has straightened, Dalia now, much better. Tough, she grew up in hardship, stern, but the one who looks out, cares about others.

It was luck that brought them together, at a time of much uncertainty. Where they were? Where life would take them? At his side, she was, through the trials and the hunger that captures.

The body and mind that weakened,
Dalia, her courage, strengthened.
What would have happened?
Without her support.
Patrice cannot, even think about.

Marcel

Marcel he would always think as smiling, care free, as they say, happy go-lucky. As he goes about one day to the next uncomplicated. His simple ways, and the trust that place by those around him. Nothing's a threat, the jubilant one good with his hands, very creative. As Sister would say, he is blessed. In his late teens, he is strongly built. Build or repair anything, the church, the school, the roof and floor, the windows finally secure.

Painted red, the front door, welcoming he says, just to make sure. The priest that visits, the people at service, all admire his courage. His drive, excellence he strives, at whatever he does. Has taken on jobs, repairs mostly, the parishioners would seek out.

The son, helper, handyman needed.
Visits, spends and finds time.
Always the one, everyone wanted.
Cooks, feeds, and welcomes him.

Back to the Slums

Thus far, everything and everyone is in check, Cap, his siblings and Sister Beatrix. The twelve years that separate, the many miles, the journey he did take, must return now, to locate. The trip is dangerous still, Lillianne insist, with him she must make. Patrice discourages and Bosco says no, he alone must go. It is his destiny, it is what he created, the course he charted, he must fulfil entirely. He is hugged by his friend, and his girlfriend, they are both his compadres. Take good care of yourself and return to us safely. Lillianne cries, but let's go, his eyes says, he must go.

Who knows what he shall find in the slums? His journey embark, by bus, truck, car or van. Walk if he must, find his way, back to those who cared for him. When he was no one, nothing now can stop him. Looks up to the sky, what he aimed for and now going. Promises himself he will make amends, hope they forgive, not knowing.

The slum has changed, now many more roads, tracks and passages. Shacks upon shacks, taller buildings they created.

Polluted, still dirty he remembers, smelly when it pours, it rains, the run-offs and the drains. No one he knows, no sign of friendlies, except for the smiles of the young girls. Reflects his face, also because of his pleasantness.

He asks around, Loraine first, whereabouts, anyone knows.

A well attired gentleman, peculiar somehow, about that age considered senior now.

My dear sir, he politely he asks, are you familiar with the Shepard's Children? With the one called Loraine? She is very good looking, you must know that face, you will never forget, once you have met. Shocks him, yes my son, I do know her very well. She now has an office, just outside the slum. My, how the organisation has grown, she now runs.

You know her, you should be proud. She has taken it leaps and bounds.

She is now the most respected, they all go to her, even the government. Foreigners, Save the Children. The first cross, is it, no, the Red Cross, yes, that one. I get mixed up, age and all, the dementia that messes, my thoughts and hunger mixes. Be happy you are not amongst us, not a clue who he was. I once lived here, Patrice said, but I got out. This is no place to live, to grow up, he said. I am glad that you did, lucky for, who smiled on you?

As politely he greeted, he said goodbye. Take care sir, to your health and to the good times, but, the bad times I hope you forget, quietly he said.

As he makes his way, the place he once played. Cannot forget that day, when he decided once and for all, to make his escape. The place where he sat, it brings memories, comes rushes back. Thoughts of hopelessness and the hunger, its accompaniment. Never enjoyment, lost feelings and disenchantment. What could not put in words back then? Now makes so much sense.

As he is making his way out the slum, he looks back, and hopes for the last time. It is important to remember where he came from, always with purpose, Patrice marches on. It did some doing, but he finally locates the building, stands adjacent to shopping complex, if you can call it. Atop the few steps that rises from the street's pavement, leads to the door that was opened. The gate inside that locks, which he shakes and knocks.

Someone answers, who is it? Just one second. Not sure what to expect, from behind the gate she steps. Just as he remembers, her face has not changed one bit. She seems smaller for some reason, for he has grown big. It is me, Patrice, she puts on her glasses and takes a closer look. As both their pores raised, she opens the gate and with him embraced. What happened? Here I thought you were dead, you and Marcel just disappeared.

I don't know what to say, but stupidly I would, I guess we moved on. I am sorry we made you worry, an understatement she said, I cried every day. Is Marcel okay? Yes he is, you would be so proud. And you, went to school? Asked expectantly, yes I completed university. With these two words, the flood gates opened, she cries and again hugs him. You have made it, I am so happy that you did, you are one of the few it is very rare. What about Mama Nieve and the children, Patrice asked. They moved out years ago, I heard she started a sewing business in a small town, I am so relieved he says.

What about you, did well? I did, so I see. I am also happy for you, your heart so full of kindness, deserves it. I never forgot when you looked out, you were always there for me, night and day, guided and helped me.

This is why I am here today.
Thank you, for all that you have done.
Know, that your work was not lost.
If you ever need courage, think of me.
What, you have created.
What, you did made me.
I will never forget you.
Shall always be indebted.
As long as I shall live.

Chapter Sixteen

The Project

Patrice returns from the slums, he finds his way back to the ones. To those who now care about him, to those who show their love. His mind for the very first time is relieved, he has accomplished everything that he had set out, has now achieved. Now on to big business, who knows what this is? He thinks, maybe high politics. What now occupies his mind, fills his thoughts, not any more personal, once it was.

However, confusion in mind he has retained. The state of the country, over the decades, nothing has changed. Politics as usual, feudal, outdated and fratricidal, he knows too well what it entails. Countries vast, some small, they all want to know for their many problems, the cause. From again occurring prevent, not so for many, they choose instead, corruption, stagnation and under-development, holds them down, prevalent.

The Congo, not the exception, but added problems. Widespread, and in the East, atrocities, soldiers retreating, and rebels advancing. In Katanga, under the guise they target civilians. Soldiers rampaging, if they can do it, so can we, the M-23. Loot shops and homes, murder, rape young girls, and women old. In Goma, nothing sacred, police and doctors even punished, shelling, bombing, blow up civilians, their neighbour would supply the weapons. Support the battalion and forcibly recruit children. Cross border to die, never know why, understand the significance, why the belligerence, in land not their forefather's.

Did they see, did they not care? Now the eyes of the world, on Rwanda takes hold. Drain on budget, the largest contingent, the Nations must apply pressure and prevent, blinds no more, what lent.

Denounce, suspend.
Kigali must show.
The blue eyed.
The black eye.
The hurt felt.
The blow.

Pulled back.
How, he lost.
M-23 crushed.

The month did take, day, hour, second, they suffered loss, retreat between their feet, just goes to show, their fight? Nobody knows. November fifth announced their wish, end of armed rebellion, months of skirmish. Return to their homes, Uganda, Rwanda, deep in the forest somewhere. By far the greatest threat, the demised paved way for others to emerge. The many heads, one cut off, the snake returns. In every province, death and destruction by guns, small and light weapons. And yes, by the most worldly-wise, degrade and defile.

Local defence turned militia, makes no sense, when does it end? The Congo Nduma Defense, against whom, what, its own country, its own people? Especially cruel, Sheka would have his day in court. The system judicial, the process, the wheels turns slowly now makes progress. Took too long to bring to justice, those who commit mass atrocities, and wide scale abuses. By this we can be sure, the tension never diffuses. The will, political it seems, moral it has always been. For many years, they did not lift finger, but armed instead. Part thereof the problem, they just allowed them to kill each other. Pick up the pieces where they left off, find another and make them suffer.

For years will continue, the violence, impunity ever more pervasive, centric and ethnic. Now the Allied Democratic Forces, Uganda originate, the invading force some call terrorists. The light you flash must focus on, not as difficult as you might think, to figure out the actors, their motives, what they hope to achieve and the dynamics. The fallout, the consequences, separate what confuses. The sick patient, the single disease, for the many problems the causes. The many symptoms would treat, a single dose, diagnosis. Ethnic polarisation, the differences, know what they must do and how to manage it.

Patrice has long figured out what they must do. National politics is fraught with danger, it just may be too much for them to handle. They think, we could start local and see where it gets you. Decentralisation, it has always been about, start from the bottom and work your way up. Have tried every style, they call it governance, countries has, comeuppance. Would never admit in fault they exist, say they were wrong, dictatorship. Call it what you must, junta, military, annihilist. Work it out, be the change, national unity could bring. How to start? Where to go? The place when lost, from the beginning.

They know that they can never change things from above,

the minds and the will of the people. There would start from if able, work on the ground, at the grassroots level. Human needs provide, build peace and stabilise. Continue momentum, up you go, step by step, the ladder you climb takes you. Build by baby steps, greater the needs and resources are too little. Finding the solutions is the greatest gamble, work with donors and partners, all those willing to help you.

Do they change course? As they talk amongst themselves, they think like no one else. Where it all begins, they have already started, so then it makes no sense. They have already laid down, time to expand. No longer only peace, but what they think is now sustainable. Patrice the architect, Bosco the muscle, Lillianne does her part equal and level, they never say follow. Gender equality, stamp out discrimination, her mainstay, her bread and butter, what she has fought for. Some would say its women's business, the patriarchal system, men never mixes. It's not about the sexes she often argues, anyone could be a victim.

They realise, they should not get carried away. What they see, the national stage at play. Heads down eyes up, focus on results. What is important? Peace and development, never power. They must move beyond politics, the black stain that soaks and grips, holds you down and drags you in. It is all about those who can use you, their thoughts on greed, only to win, never about the people. What it must be about, they have lived, still does. What their needs are, livelihood, security, shelter, health and education, who knows better? Impossible in the land of millions, all those who need. How to approach? Stupendous the problem, seems.

How would they approach the subject? Look for clues, how should they go about it. Forget about power and politics, access to government resources. Patrice is not alone, the thoughts that swirls, dizzy at times, his head hurts. He shares with his girlfriend, soon wife to be, bonded in love not only. The new chief Bosco, well he also wants a miracle. The state of the country, concerns, consumes them. Their imagination overtime works, how to solve this problem?

Politics now, they have discounted and forgotten. Patrice thinks, to build a big house, a mansion believe in. Resources are too little, but millions needed. Start from the bottom, the foundation, the strength, the test time survives, matters not the length. Build on top, and build again, until completed. No more will be needed, the mansion you have always wanted, you have now created. We will start from the bottom, Patrice says. We will work with the community, independently, bring back some sanity. Every model we shall use, a trickle up approach, if you so choose. Call it what you must, good fortune, luck, shall shine upon us. Work for the people, there is no greater cause, there is no greater struggle.

If there is a god.
She would say?

Man have to decide.
By humanity he lives, survives.
Perpetuate, he must.
Lapsarian, I am not.
I still believe.
In you trust.
The fall, has not.
Do what you must.
Your specie survive.

The bond connects.
Invisible it is.
Feels at times.
Until felt.
The hurt inside.
How can it be?
Most of the country suffers daily?
No hope for the future.
Dreams you all have.
What makes them different?
Yourself, must ask.
Humanity, the chain.
You must believe in.
What connects, the bond?
As strong, the link.
When weak.
Shall drag 'all' in.

Yet you make, create ways.
To keep them down.
Segments large, population.
All ships rise, big, small.
The tide that brings.
Currents strong.
Development for all.
Not only some.
To be rich.
There must be poor.
A stupid calculation.
For...sure.
Businessmen, world leaders.

All believe, the concept.
But how can you be rich?
When there is so much poor.
Who will support you?
Buy what you build.
How can this be?
Common sense.
Bretton Woods.
Teaches you.
But, for you
Can work, certainly.
Dependency, the lord of all
Absolutely.

Bosco knows all about land issues and displacement. Patrice, about poverty, peace and development. Lillianne, about gender and children. She majored in psychology at the university, has worked with an international agency. She has understudied one of the most brilliant Congolese psychologist, would emerge, as she did, with tremendous understanding. She has witnessed first-hand, the trauma and effects, conflict and violence has on women and children. As they set about, for their plan is not unique, hundreds before have done it, in every conflict zone, on every continent.

They check, have we? Covered every possibility and emergency. It does not matter, we will repeat. It is not a competition, wish all could do it. The organisation is non-governmental, would illicit help, wherever they could find.

Raise funds on the ground, online, what the hell, do whatever it takes even beg. Do what they must, for them not, the people would trust. What would they name it? How would they represent all the people? The 'Congolese People Project' that says it, not restricted, but all inclusive.

No politicians, all else welcomes. Every tribe, clan, could lend a hand, they would call, utopian. Never mind who says, we are here to help. Spread the message, anyone can do it.

Who needs politicians or state resources? They have never been there, here, or, anywhere. All they know is how to create division, feed their own, and starve the rest of the nation. It does not matter, Patrice says. We will starve with them, live with and feel their pain. The sacrifice we must make, the promises made. They all now share, make the country great, at any cost, the dirtier we get, better. In makeshift tents sleep, do what we must to gain their trust.

Lillianne and Bosco does not know how.

Patrice knows too well.

They must draw up a plan, how should they approach? Deal with each condition. They will start at home, always first, where charity begins all have been taught, to everyone, well known. In Katanga, many parts still restive, they must get in, connect and establish, with the warlord, rebels, armed groups and not. The Army command, state claim, rights, but not demand, the mighty holds in hand. The people's corridor, create space, access humanitarian. Patrice plans, but still young man, Bosco a chief, respect command. Very ticklish, the issues sensitive, would they listen? What do they respect? What do they have in common? But religion, what connects?

A senior Catholic priest, known for his good deeds, his whole life has worked towards building peace. Always in front when things go wrong, has risked his life many times to stabilise. When violence erupts between the warring factions. The brave one, a man of the people, always in front. He does not care, would take a bullet, if he must. Protect those he loves, save the lives of the innocent. In his god he does, the people in him trust. In his late sixties strong, his skin dark brown, the sun comes from. He is lean, tall and imposing, his voice booming, he speaks all listens.

Would he agree? If we asked him to broker, they asked one another. Between us and them, the people now depend. What would he say? Would he warn us about getting in the way? The three are hesitant. Patrice says: what would it hurt, the door, look for another, when one closed. On moral high ground we stand, what we seek is only good. Righteous we have been, and so we remain, and the righteous would agree. Bosco musters the courage, and the language, intelligent and non-technical. The father seemed shocked, as no local before have attempted. Such an intervention, the scale and magnitude, they are proposing.

How would you go about? The father asked, interested. We would start small, Bosco said, Patrice and Lillianne listen in. On their tongues, they can taste it, the nervousness, they do not understand, why the sweaty palm? Approval needed, confidence, on the brink, they can grab it. Now, you have my attention, come into my office, Jean Claude beckons. I have a couple hours before service, I will give this time to you, to convey your message.

Before you begin, I want you to understand, I have worked with, and met with many individuals and organisations. All with plans, mandates they call it, solid they all seem, as if made with concrete. In black and white lines, even between would read. I am not here to judge, I just want to understand. The Father looks at Lillianne then Bosco. Looking down, your father would never forgive me, if you get into any trouble. He looks at Patrice, you young man, seems very capable. I must still look out for you all, understandable? What makes you different or better? Would your plan work? Did not before with another.

This is exactly what, Patrice says, our plan is not a cast in concrete. In black on white, the ink that dries, cannot erase, replace? We do not answer to a board, donor, or sponsor. We have no director, a country manager who sits with Minister, explain our presence, work within parameters. We may be poor, do not have access to millions, Toyotas, four wheeled, communications, satellite feed. But what we do have is experience, born, bred, lived it, came from it, still in it. Our hopes and dreams are not transferrable. No one can understand, replace our mission, it must be only, by our hands.

I would allow Patrice to continue, if it is okay with you, I ask you respectfully. There is no need to be so formal, Bosco. I baptised you, have known you from a baby, you called me uncle. Your family have been so generous to the church and me, it is now my duty, to repay the kindness your family has always shown to me. Patrice takes his cue, starts to lay out the plan, says, forgive me if I sound arrogant. We just want you to understand as we do. We have been in this situation for so long, now everyone wants to help. The foreigners have taken so much, now they knock at the door. From one hand they took, now from the other will give. They wish to help, fix what they have broken. What they bring, resources they spend. Is nothing but a gesture, token!

It would never be enough, what they have taken from us, left in this place severed. It hurts, no words can express, the loss, grief we possess, the stigma we carry, no fault of ours. They pitted us against each other, brother against brother. They blame us now that we do not know better. But we do, those of

212

us we see, accepts our differences, we believe in humanity. We know what separates us? The causes many. When we attempt to build, they say we are not good enough. Even our own would never trust us, only the outsiders. Who knows better? The things we need to rebuild, the family, the community, the state, where to begin.

Father Jean Claude stops Patrice, having said all that you did, I am now convinced. I will broker a deal between you and the various factions. They may not understand peace, but, they know the problems, that they are part of. The suffering of the people, they had a hand.

I am sure you will get the access you seek, reach the ones, most in need. Please tell me more, how will you achieve. The course you have set out, and how can you be sure?

Chapter Seventeen
The Work of Beings

For what would sound like a prayer, looking at Jean Claude, thank you father, Patrice would say. But, he never did, prayed, that is. All that time he went to church, along with Sister Beatrix and the other kids. It confused him, how do you believe in something, when all he has ever seen? The cross, the crucifix, the pictures on the wall. And the hymns that they sing, who was it for, all? It seemed funny, sometimes, even strange, he smiled mostly while his ear ringed.

He remembers his mother, what she told him so long ago. I will look down on you from the sky, be never afraid, you, I will guide. So he did, he prayed to his mother, for him there was no other, no god, pantheon, or saviour. That was it, the smile on his lips. Some thought he was possessed, talking to spirits, that he was touched in the head. He believes, felt and connects. The bond that was made stronger, the angel, the saint, once his mother.

Patrice now, has an overwhelming sense of confidence in the Father, Yes! That one. He reminds of Sister Beatrix, his belief and pleasantness, standing tall, uprightness. People like you, Patrice says, gives us hope, that there is good in the world. He realises about Jean Claude, he is not trying to make things difficult. He just wants to make sure, that we know what we are about. By this he shows that he cares. If I had one wish, would be to predict, Patrice says. But I do not and cannot, that is why in you we now trust.

Our wish to do well, you so should measure our approach. You are the vessel to help carry out, the barometer, the crystal ball.

What if we told you? We do not have everything figured out, money very little. Would you still help us? Would you be able? To put aside your strict approach, the sanctity sometimes goes beyond the church. Your flock all around, everywhere to be found. Jean Claude nods his head, you are right Patrice, he said. You have made your point clear, and I must say very well. Now spell it out, your approach every step of the way. We all have our areas said Patrice, expertise you might say. Displacement, peace, gender, healing, and education. You know all this, but first we must create a space for the displaced to return.

Pick up the pieces so to speak, what they left so hastily. Fled the violence, on their heads brought down, all measure of impunity. They had no choice, if they stayed they would be dead. Most times, slow and agonising, witness friends, family and neighbours bludgeoned. The horrors they have seen, witnessed, some may never come back home again. Would be their dream, for the many return to the place childhood, to the place of birth. The land, the house, the shack, inherited through generations, now get back. In the bushes, between the trees they would play. Brings back memories, time of not worry, not of danger, imagination only, the limit of behaviour.

The next step is to convince them. How do they return, the place once called home? They are innocent, in the game, it matters not for them. Who wins or loses, they just want to live, carry on their business, whatever it is? Plan their daily lives, plant their gardens, tend to their livestock, just feed their children. The bane of their existence, armed conflict, for the forcefully displaced. Their problems multiplies with every bullet that fires. A notch on the belt, every square foot of land, they get for themselves. Among the population, hardest hit are those displaced. Forced from their homes, travel long distances alone. Women and young girls, travel by night, for refuge in search. Has lost everything, their dignity remains, then to be taken. Men, their little boys, assets lost. Cannot plan or figure out? Their future now gone, what they have built, has run its course.

This is perhaps our biggest problem, who knows this better than you father. You have witnessed since independence, all of our mistakes, we only destroy, shatter. Our vision, our dreams, would always falter. We break down, never build, how do we fix this situation? So many vulnerable, weak, sleep on the streets. Move from one place to the other, puts pressure on our neighbour. I know we are not alone, in South Sudan, Ethiopia, Syria and South America. Why would they help us? What caused our problems? Who created the situation? The Sub-Saharan, who cares what happens?

And what can be caused, we must still try to figure out. The damage to the economy, of livelihoods lost. We are always rebuilding, going nowhere fast. Every step we take, must start again, we are pushed back. We are at that time, we see a change coming, perhaps for us the new beginning.

The stage, the transition one man rule they see ending, what would it mean? What true democracy might bring? Two thousand fourteen, sixteen is fast approaching. We should start, get going and hit the ground running. It is important yes, who wins, but steadiness and leadership is what we favour. Anyone we support must bring stability, benefits for the people favourably.

We must continue with our plan, be there for those, give a helping hand. Patrice was sure, they cannot be wrong. They are all on board, the concept all they have learned, would now carry out, for all whom it may concern. The people, their cause, they will be the champion. The problems inherit, for the many who witness, they will be the first to end it.

The first step we need your help, Patrice's plea to the Father. The commitment from the warring factions that they would not trouble, but leave alone the people. It would be in their favour, if it ever comes up, the matter. Things are changing, circumstances are now different. For those now are held to account, for the violence they have committed, to civilians and non-combatants, would now pay. The price heavy, life in jail, the reputation unwanted, for rape, murder, recruiting child soldiers, what no one wants.

If they have one ounce of humanity, self-respect and dignity. They would prevent, find ways to protect the innocents. Most end up in The Hague, equally treated, or their worst fear, life in a Congo cell, mistreated. We must convince them, that this is not what they want. History remembers, it does not forget, all those who have helped, takes not kindly to those who did not. Their names go down into the annals of history, all men wants to be great, remembered for all the good things they did, not blood thirsty scoundrel, bandit.

Their children, their future generations carry it, the shame they will feel, in guilt they live and reel. In retrospect we must look at it, who can take pride? When they look it looks back, the mirror reflects, not a man greatness, but madness. Their hands cuffed as they walk to the court, smiles for their supporters. The crowd swells and cheer, the jubilant mob knows not better. Every day and night anguished in thoughts, the suffering they have caused. The lives they have taken haunts them, inside this what have made? What now carries them? What life could have been?

They would then wonder, about what they have taken in their quest for power.

Consider if it applies jus in bello, the rules of engagement are there to follow, never laid out, but all they know. Makes no difference, the soldier of fortune, rebellious dissident, and to the people misfortune. Must lay down and die, this is what they expect, hapless resort, stand up and show resistance. Caught in the middle, when they defend, now they are one of them. Make them your friend, this is what we say. One day they will stand with you, we will show you the way. This the key where we begin, the road we pave, the wide avenue we create, the great opening. It all begins with support, however difficult, bring on board, or be left out.

When circumstances change, the time we all see coming. They will be remembered, now things have changed, they pitched in. Played their part, laid down their weapons and created the path. We are not the government, we do not work for any international agency. We do not work for the UN, our work regulated by any policy, INGO we copy only. We cannot give assurances, immunities or rewards, but we are witnesses from this point on. The good that they do, regardless how little we will swear to. It is all about change, they can all be part of it. The season brings nothing stays, the winds of change no one can resist it.

Their kind for years have used, leaves them all now so

confused. What they would do now wonder, if they follow their hearts, the mind will along that wander. The Warlord, the General and the Militia leader. He must now all convince, take into the field. Jean Claude understands, has laid it out, the plan he spells for them. For each can be the people's champion, now they understand, towns and villages no battle should inflict. The people, they did not choose to be in it. The father will oversee, respect they have always had for him and presently. Place an observer in every village, wear the shirt with the insignia on it.

They will all respect the sacred oath made on this day. November the first, you have our word, each one would say. Diplomacy that works, the Father shuttles between each, and every day. They commit to this in writing, not to peace between, but a truce with the people. Attacks will stop there will be no more running out. They can come back to their lives, no longer do they need hide. They now have assurances, they are committed, may they never go against it? The Father realises he is now in this, cannot come out even if he wants. He feels committed, what he always wanted, but did not know how? For him heaven sent, the master plan if there was ever one. He feels great beyond measure, invincible now, the people's saviour.

The flock returns, the shepherd has now his children. In far fields they strayed, did not know they would return this way. To each his own agenda, it worked out that way. The priest has his, we too, Bosco would then say. We all want the same thing, but for different reasons, we are not different, Patrice says. We do not share common cause, upstage the government that's what we do. Bring back the congregants, his church well to do. What is wrong with that? We scratch each other's back.

Now that this is all settled, we shall spread the word, it is time for them to return home. Pick up the pieces, we will help you rebuild homes, help with livelihoods lost. The lives that was lost no one can replace, but we will help ease the pain, Lillianne will manage somehow.

You know what? What we think often about, even if we had a lot, it would never be enough. The day spent to destroy, would take years to rebuild, easy to break hard to build. Gone in a second, centuries old monuments civilisations the same, remembers only the name. What we can provide, with both hands offer. We know they will appreciate, from which tribe we come, who cares? We are all the same colour, brother helping brother. Thus begins the work of beings, humans that is. The ones who recognises, understands what must be done, the salvation of the people, those in need of help and healing.

The first village they come upon, strewn personal effects on the ground. Signs of people escaping hastily, no plans on returning. A small vegetable stall broken, kicked, pushed with the foot down. What it once held, where it fell, now dried blackened by the heat of the sun. Huts burnt almost to the ground, the timber remains, the narrow wood from small trees stood. In dirt caked, the mud baked from the fire they placed. The sorrow it brings, what men do each other? Only because they could, no reason other.

It is not hard, it is simple, we have what we need, ample. We will just start with what we have. The villagers now present, looks at them, not in amusement nor bewilderment. Get the twigs hold together, say, makeshift brooms, the remnants of hate must sweep away, wherever they may lay. Gather wood and branches, the strip of forest, the children would get away, once they played.

Bosco starts, he lays down the rules and plans, and about engagement, associating with outsiders. We will rebuild the huts, he says, Lillianne says no way. What comes first is the school, we will build the next day. Where would the children stay? You did not let me finish. The children were first on my mind. Bosco is sometimes impatient, help me he beseeched. Patrice would then say something so obvious! Everything at this point is important, you are both right. But we must have our priorities straight, we must create safe environment, in this case housing takes preference. As soon as they are settled, we will build the school I promise. This was good enough for Lillianne, her smart husband, the plan he has always.

As the three would consult with each other, sometimes under the sunshine, at times under the stars, with little or no light. Unsure at times, what would be their next step? But for one thing they can be sure, whatever happens? They cannot fail, for all they have eyes on them. As the word got out, their network, circle, those they associated with at the university. Who had along with them struggled!

They once together fought for something, wanted to now all pitch in. Many from well to do families, not wealthy, very poor some, they would all agree, whatever they can bring, would surely.

The team has now gotten bigger, many more wants to be an observer. Patrice tells them that they can work and observe at the same time, we all are. They have printed shirts now, 'Congolese People' in white the rest bright red.

The most generous supporter, a heart of consciousness donated. It did take a few weeks, the weather permitted. All done huts, the school completed, surroundings white washed, even the stones that lined the place. The villagers most subsistence farmers, lives off earthy provisions, rare a few chickens. A sense of normality returns, a little support all they yearned.

This is but only the first, many more remains. Create the reputation that precede, to the point they no longer need to beg and plead. With an NGO would partner, help with sanitation and water. Gives added momentum, with confidence to move onward, forward. Hundreds of villages, remote cut off from access. As they did at university they have now created model, one they hope all will follow. Most important they realised, they created for the people, space, a place to live and life that is safe. Proudly wear their shirts, emblazoned, the sign the badge of honour well deserved. Some doubted, the sceptics, some waited and observed would fall, just wished them well, deep down inside, all.

Months, as if the wind had gone, the many villages visited. To some have not returned, the people moved on, disappeared who knows what happened? Signs of what happened too hard to mention. When asked they close their eyes, shake their heads, it is very sad. They are strained, their good must now take, with the bad they gave. Must now wipe away, must forget? They are pained.

As they have moved from village to village, they have with villagers bonded, the many met along the way, with them banded. No doubt the word have spread, the people now look out and welcomes them. They number now twenty one, once only three, have done splendidly. All university trained, a few finishing, specialists they are in many fields, agriculture, nutrition and engineering. Psycho-social support they have reinvented, all now pitches in which helps with healing. Each village now has a school, make shift it may be, many can sit. The child, learn to read and write, count from one to ten, from

A to Z learn to spell. In each a designated teacher, spends the day, keeps them going astray. Sit, talk, council and support. Tells them stories, they laugh and play, fills the day.

Many requests comes, many NGOs wants now to join. Be part of this movement, with the Project become one. From the beginning they have said, it is not a competition, all are welcome. Indigenous they belong, their approach needs not approval. An umbrella may be called, one that covers all. Lay out the plan, lead the way and show them all how it is done. Two years now have gone, their experience has surpassed, have moved beyond expectations. Many more now seek their intervention.

Have gained respect beyond measure, they are trusted, the people's saviour, the service provided. The force seems to be reckoned. Has gone out, time to go national, the church remains, Jean Claude reign in. The church they all respect,

Jean Claude keeps them in check. Any sign infractions, the Father pull up. Observers on the ground, they do not, would not, test their luck. Everyone is talking about the 'Congolese People' Project. Where it started out, from humble beginnings, the bold step. The lumps in their throats, now clear when they approach. No more sweaty palms, the hand that shake, firm now the grip, the impression they make.

With confidence, step by step. Draw up the plan, put it down on paper, official will now be, anyone wants to see. What they have made, what they have created, a model to take every town and village. A plan of action designed to take into consideration. All what the people have lost, help them bring back come about. Repair and make right what was wrong? All they have done, even the government, do not point fingers, for they cannot. Come to terms, must fix and move on.

Vengeance they must forget, Patrice introduces the concept. How to avoid conflict, live with their neighbours in peace not tarnish. The new module for school, it is the only way, Patrice would say. The old does not learn, they are stuck in their ways, the young does not see like this. To build a new country, must start from the ground not the other way around. Thus we shall with children, we must prevent, the sure means circumvent. Find solutions to obstacles, the young it seems are always willing and able.

Not for one second believe that they have not noticed. Those in authority, those from the government. From what they know, they have taken interest. They are watching to see how far it goes, but will not interfere. The government does not want them to fail, in fact, they are happy for the help.

What, they could not.

For them, great success.

Chapter Eighteen
His Presence explains

They have worked very hard, their tails off you might say. Many times half starved, hunger in their stomachs, to none dismay. At night they slept on the dirt, sparked the firewood, the bugs and mosquitos drives away. Under open night sky, witnessed one time only, shoots the body and then fade away. The rest of the stars many, looks down on them now only, as they count and drift away. The many projects called interventions. The people on them depend, relied on them. Prepared for what would come, the expectation that one day would reach, would not be too long, better would get. The day will come, have grown strong.

The conditions people face, they always look with regret, to the future, a better time now face and expect. They all feel coming, for the many years disappointed. All the promises that no one could deliver, the corruption in every nook and corner, from the top of government to the civil servant. Cronies handpicked, ingrained and embedded. When would they see the last of it?

Two thousand sixteen, the mandate they choose to call it, comes to an end, constitutionally and morally, all comprehend. The people look forward, democracy not by bullet, but by the reform promised. They pray for change, who knows their saviour? By the ballot box would create anyone, or the other. To deliver them from this place, to one that is better. The world has changed, still they linger in this place, everywhere there is hopelessness. In every country, its people decide for themselves, their lives, their future would find ways to change. To compromise was our mistake.

The shockwave many did not expect. Is it that there are not ready for it? The cancellation of elections, not ready to step down. Relinquish power, can hold on no longer. Set up the succession plan, when the next takes over. His right hand man install, fooled them once, twice, not at all. Not in place would have to wait. Their greatest fear, what he did, Pierre? In Burundi sectarian violence triggered, when they played with, what they tried to upend. The constitution manipulate, the new one could not defend.

The government argues, they did not cancel, it is but a mere adjournment, an unexpected deferment. Patrice, Bosco, Lillianne and the others, all shook their heads in disappointment. Nothing surprises them in this place. Just when they thought all things will be different from this point forth, the benefit would give to him no doubt. The bull horn, in many a forum, even argued in court. The opposition vent, but they cannot reverse decision. For two thousand and eighteen, we shall just have to wait. The opposition gets stronger, and the people gets louder.

Afraid of what would happen, if this is indeed a trick. The many villages and towns burned in Burundi and Cameroon. The Congo, the box, ethnic hatred, the tinder filled, strike a match burn at will. They hope and pray that this must never happen here. The suffering and strife, for the many years they survived. They think the final nail, will he destroy what remains? This will be the end, the road to hell. Then we will know, just how they feel, all those countries that goes up in flames.

What to do, but back to square one. Bosco feels a great sense of pity, expressed openly. Not for himself but his beloved country. Only a chief, from where he stands would see. As if they have lost the chance to get back what they have taken. The chance to rebuild what they have broken.

Bosco feels numb inside, turns to Patrice whom confides.

This the game of politics, the first words from his lips. And yes they have taken it too far, I know just how you think. As they continue the debate, Patrice nails it, whatever they can do, they will do, if they can get away with it, but no one is immune. The system is alive breathing, they can keep it down for generations sometimes, but certainly not for all the time. Things are changing, we see happening. All over the world, right here soon coming. One thing for sure, my bottom dollar if I was betting, they can never come back once we get rid of them.

All the things they have done, all the problems they have caused. All the right thinking people, by them shall not return. How do you know such things? Bosco asks of Patrice, he says: it is not only hope, but common sense. People get the government they deserve, we are the ones who make it happen we are the ones who will it. However, anything can change if the majority wants it. You know what, even you can predict the future. Just think very hard on it, I realise so must you. Think about it, believe it, it must come through. He has taken the first step, if he changes his mind, history would not be too kind. On him and his kind. What they all want, the title of life president.

What gives them that right? Rule over people and their lives. Their entire life, decides who dies or who survives, who eats, who gets the job, who gets the education? Their children all go to private boarding schools in Switzerland, France and Belgium. They shop and eat at expensive restaurants, as they mingle with the best, they get a world class education. Our children want to learn, they try to read as they stifle in the heat, under sheds built of galvanise and straw. The ones that we built, for the ones they ignore.

To be god it seems, the depth their dreams. We must remind them that they are not, absent, invisible, so is he. We cry for help, not even presidents, only people those who are able, the helping hand they put out raise you up. On your knees you beg wait for help, some they come those who forget, the colour of your skin, the tribe belong in the human being is all that is seen. The incredible journey, all that we have done, all we have been through. The road, the trail, however difficult has brought us, trials we have faced to reach this point still does not become. Who knows if we do? To where do we belong? We are left to our fate, by the destiny for us they create. Tell us our needs, what we should not have and our wants, how much, however little, is enough?

A drop in the bucket only, or so the saying goes. Have not escaped them, as they think and worry, the displaced so many. The lives that they have touched, they believe very little. Time to spread the word go out seems a better way to reach out. Their workforce are but small, that a single intervention can take months. How can they possible achieve, reach all those in need. All the villages and communities around the country, upheaval and distress tears them apart. Relentless the cause, they have no control, must find ways to stem the flow.

But good news that travels fast, sometimes lightning speed. Might be the best way to resolve this predicament. For the thousands have heard about the project, now they all want to replicate. The hope it will work out, would be their dream, with the solution in hand, intervene. They will need to know how to go about this. The plan not as simple as they might think. How with armed groups negotiate, the gangs and the state. They have intervened in over twenty villages thus far, across this state, the province of Katanga, many more to go must now cover.

Reprisals and skirmishes down, but many areas are still very dangerous. In the East mostly a few Central. Pockets of violence, those who show resistance. The ADF has been weakened, the state forces have almost beaten. Across the country, they return, the displaced to the life that awaits, they must do our part. The United Nations assists, things are changing, a sense of peace fragile but holding. Peace this is all they need, enough to stimulate just enough confidence in the system. Security, law and order between the borders.

Should they consider? For all the challenges they face. Should they stay? Or move to the east that is unsafe? In the west the violence continues. Hundreds of victims, the armed conflict continues. The FDLR, hindrance to peace upsets, continue the course, the UN, FARDC, the joint force. The masses, this land so vast cannot cover. Alarm that sound the call, the group insists do not risk it all. Patrice and Bosco takes heed, Lillianne would join in and plead. It is true what they say, in this zone that is safe we should indeed stay. They have worked so hard to achieve this little piece, peace, why chance, do not go out. Invite all to come and see, it is not perfect but closest can come to it.

So they did, in the weeks that followed there were several

visits. Social groups and community activists, even some from another church. Most surprising, a government official came inquiring. Can we replicate this model? He asked of Bosco, who said: You can surely. But, I would let Patrice speak, he knows more about peace. The first element in the quest for development. It is he that worked out the plan to bring back the people. Then I, how to enhance, build back their lives, bring back a sense of community and settlement.

Patrice takes his cue, and, from where Bosco left off he continues: I do not know if you have the time, or how much you can endure. To explain this concept, for it is not that simple. The advisor looks at him, you look like a smart young man, well mannered, well brought up, your parents must be so proud. A university graduate, look at all you have done, I have all day, please continue Patrice, have you say, do not leave out I want to hear. Finally Patrice would have his day. Express all that he has inside, what has been bottled up. But he knows that he must contain, do not come out fighting.

Patience, what Cap taught him, for all the years they have fought? Do not get ambitious, slowly, make you point. Make sure they understand, now they will understand everything. For now that he knows, they move away from the group. Mr. Mande, Bosco, Lillianne and Patrice find a decent space under the mango tree, the sun it shades. Arrange in a semi-circle from a tree that once stood, now just pieces of trunks, blocks of wood. This village very quiet, miles away from any bustle and traffic. Anyone can have their say, you have no choice but to listen. Even for those hard of hearing, whichever way their head turn, vibrate their eardrum, fluttering.

They rearranged the blocks now facing each other. How did you come up with such a 'scheme?' The wrong choice of word for what they discovered, looking squarely at Patrice. For what will follow is not a conversation, but a presentation, that will go one way. What he has practiced in his head for many years. What he has planned? What he would say? Would it go his way? Would he leave Mr Mande stunned? Would it Lillianne in tears? Then Bosco smiles, let him have it, give him hell. For no one has ever portrayed what life is really like, to sum up pain? To put in words what they choose, things would leave misunderstood?

Mr Mande, I thank you for the opportunity, I do not know if it would change anything if I tell you my story? Mande replies to Patrice: "I work for one of the most powerful ministers, it is by his request that I came here. He was the one who found out about you, he did all the research, handed me the file, then for you I came in search. The minister was born in a small village just like this. From birth had to run for his life, I guess you can say that he has been running ever since. He is not from this area, but his heart is in it, your cause, your struggle, that is."

Mande Continues: "You have my assurance, you all need not be suspicious. An action plan is what we seek, we do not want to take away all you have built. I want you all to know that the government wants changes. From the president, down to the civil servant. But, we do not know how to manage it. There are forces greater, some local, domestic, most of all international, foreign complicit. I will lay out, how it works." Mande continues: "If you do not continue their cause or refuse, they will replace you. If the balance of power changes, they can out you. It is all the game of greed and power, but the multinationals knows much better."

"Their governments helps, the colonials entrenched. It has never changed, only the skin, someone to do their bidding.

Secure your place when it's over, in the metropolis, live like a king among princes. It is all about to change, we can feel it coming. There will be an election next year and we must put everything is in place. The transfer of power must be done gradually, cannot upset the balance, only faces friendly. So what do you say? Are you in or out? Are you ready to make the change? But now on a national scale, on the big stage."

'So Patrice, you can continue, I did not mean to cut across. I just wanted to reassure you. That your plan is great from cover to cover I have read it. We will make it a national plan, you all can administer it. We will take it to the cabinet, adopt it and fix a budget. Put things in place and even if the government changes, no one will touch it. You all, your team, must be ready and willing. You believe, so do I, but I will still tell you, it is not easy to replicate what you did. The trust in you the people have placed. People return just because you say it is okay to. No one will trust certainly not government. Who can blame them? For they blame us. We created that environment. This is the first step I think to begin the healing. Bring back some trust, show we care for them".

They all smile, except Patrice who seems upset. He did not get a chance to vent. He did not have his say, he has been side tracked. He will have to continue some other day. Mande promises that he will get much higher audience, he would not regret. Thought they saw of him the last, but not even a week would past. For a signal they would await, the phone call Mr Mande would make. He did keep his promise after all. Find your way to the capital, do not delay, he did say. You have an audience with the minister, the president's most trusted advisor. He wants to hear your story, what led you up to, all? What inspired? And, answered to what call?

They know deep inside with elections in the air, everyone wants to appear, that they are on top of situation, they want to prove they care. What would it hurt? So what if they use? We would show them, Patrice says. Arrived in the capital, they travelled for two days straight. Mr Mande so happy to please. Provides accommodation and transportation, takes them to expensive restaurants. They are being pampered, feels like they are being buttered. They think, what they all want, the name and association. What they could give to them. What no one wanted, trust? What they have earned, the Project with sincerity and concern.

At the Minister's office, as big as some houses. Armed guards lined the halls, the corridor that leads to his door. The Minister is tall and imposing, he smiles welcoming. He is well attired, dressed for business. He says: Please have a seat at the table, looks like it is fit for a banquet. Fruits they have never seen, apples, pears and grapes green. Wine of white, red, meats fried and baked bread. Please enjoy what we prepared, actually my wife did, the Minister said. I told her all about you, and would like to meet when we are through.

Needless to say, they were all very uncomfortable, especially Patrice. My stomach feels a bit upset, he says, had not time to rest. The Minister picks up, seems more like distress, mental uneasiness, not stomach queasiness.

I much prefer to get down to business, says Patrice. I like your style, the Minister says to him with a smile. Still standing, Mande beckons Patrice to sit. Rearing to go, Patrice could not hide his impatience. The Minister says okay Patrice, he lets go. Patrice would now have his say: "I always knew that it would come a day. Sit or stand before someone, relay all that I have done. From birth all the troubles I have encountered, all the days without food. No one from government, only the few that were kind came to help. No one understands the plight of the helpless".

Mande attempts to speak, the Minister says do not disturb him. He told Patrice to go ahead, have your say, you can cry or scream. Patrice continues: "I am just one, but there are many hundreds, thousands like me, all over this land. No future, no plans, no one to look out, just orphans. I was born, grew up in the slum, I did not know what would happen, what I would become? I took the chance, I escaped from the clutches. I ended up in the jungle, a life what I thought would soon end. But as luck would have it, found my family, and the father I never had.

"Though it was hard, life was just that, I made do with what I had. But you know what? It made me who I am. I would not want it any other way. That life made me strong, tough. Made me understand, what is at the end of struggle, it is true success. Even if you were not handed, you can still achieve all that you need. With just a little help, was all that I seek".

"You will never understand unless you lived it, from hand to hand, poverty stricken. From pillar to post, or so the saying goes. Never before thought much of it, but it's true, it is where generosity takes you. Those who accepts you, takes you in, provides for you and expects the best from you. I am an orphan you can say, but for long did not stay that way. From out of the trench, the gutter I was put in, the one that was made for people like me. I know this is not your problem or concern. But it is what I think about it every night and day. The children just like me, born in absolute poverty. The minutes, hours, days, weeks, months, years, for those who enjoy life flies by in seconds. But not so for me and my others, painfully, it slowly goes by. We spend the time, we worry, where the next meal would come, in what future do we belong?"

Where did this all come from, everyone, they are all stunned. Shocked, they could have heard the pin dropped. 'You should be one of us', is all the minister could say, 'you will be a great leader someday'. "I am not quite finished, respectfully" did not mean to sound blunt' Patrice would say. The Minister intervenes: 'It is quite okay, I know you are upset it is not easy to recollect, bring up the memories, a difficult life, one you lived, perhaps still'. 'Is this why you were inspired?' The minister asked Patrice. "In a sense yes, but it goes much, much deeper, for that what was required" he answers.

"Perhaps not the topic for today, but I could give you an idea. Just what it would take to make this country better. The road when travelled, how you emerge. The leaders, the country better it will be despite poverty. A chance is what they all want, but it comes down to creating the right conditions".

Chapter Nineteen
The Audience

As the audience with the Minister continues. Patrice is in the process, still venting, in what seems never ending. His confidence grows, urged on by the supportive look of Bosco, the inviting tone of the Minister's voice, and, the awkward, shy smile of Mande. He feels fearless and strong, he is now full of confidence. He has been preparing for this for so long, for what would then come. Had everyone stunned? Patrice said bluntly, well, he said apophasistically.

"Who wants this? We were not born this way, it is why people fight, kill and steal. What I believe, I now say" intending to answer anyway. "Conditions leaders create, when you see this, just know one thing, you have failed."

Patrice continues: "Yet they continue, blames everyone. It is easy, only finger pointing, on you the rest turn, believe you are alone. The solution no, but the biggest part of the problem. You fight to stay in power, for nothing gets better, term limits extends, keeps all in wonder. Pit neighbour against neighbour, our race, tribe, brothers forced to take from each other. I get so emotional, sometimes overcome by rage, why never hate? What they try to inculcate, the weak in mind overtake, designed it is, fake."

Patrice tells them: It seems, that he has told them off, the officials not alone addressing, all in the room listens everyone. The Minister's wife has now joined, with Patrice agrees, an ally found. 'You can change all this' she tells the man, her caring husband. 'How does he see this problem?

Does no one else? Patrice answers instead: "They choose to neglect, I speak in terms generally, not blaming anyone particularly. You are the first to take this step". To the Minister then said. Do you understand how I feel? Red his eyes, swollen and watery. Anger he has carried all his life, with every step doubt, it now comes out. Why are they all, why do they look so surprised? Mande moue, control taken away, now subjected to.

Patrice looks at them, not a single word, nothing they utter. Bosco, Lillianne privileged, they grew up wanting nothing. The Minister once poor, guess he suffered, his wife who knows. Mande not sure, a bureaucrat does not just spring up, but sympathetic they know, displayed the first time they met and continues to grow, why? Does not know? They must be all on the same page by now, so they say, it now seems after all. It just might go his way, if even one he manages to convince, maybe things will change. A dream for sure, who would listen to this boy so poor? Brought up on the wrong side, nothing and no one, no parent influential.

What he did, what he helped create? Has brought him here, to this place. The halls of power, the helper, the saviour. "We do not have to be, all, should now realise, a killer. To be great, to reach this place." Patrice said. "This makes so much sense to me." said the Minister, he continues: "but you know, we know this already, it is difficult, the restrains placed on us. There is so much competition, it is difficult to alleviate the problem, believe me, I know of what you speak. Believe me when I say that I have tried, the influence it seems, beyond these walls, lies. For so long, decades passed, we have governed by force, must admit, it now comes back on us."

The Minister: "Demands are made, and by force they take, for there is left nothing, for you the poor. We can never give assurances, the current climate restricts it is only for the privileged. The competition too great, you must understand, you cannot depend on the government. If you can find no solution to the problem. Maybe, you can go around, find a better way for the situation to overcome". Bosco answers. 'I can say precisely what the problem is. Competition for state resources, why they would all kill. This I have witnessed many a time in my dealings with the government." Patrice agrees: "we must find a way to circumvent, find donors, organisations, anyone willing to help. The United Nations even, we cannot wait, we cannot waste any time. The people, the children their lives depend. Where we must the place it all starts, at the household and community level, win minds and hearts."

Continues Patrice: "At every level these conditions exist. We must approach from every point of vantage. With haste eliminate, then propagate". The Minister all this time with a smile on his face. "You are so enthused," he says. "Do not mean to burse your bubble, but I was once like you. Hot and strong headed, ready to take on the world. Until I stepped into it, this world I am now part of maintains control. It keeps your feet, on the ground, firmly planted, prevents you from drifting into the clouds. You may not get it, there is nothing tingling, develop that cold feeling. The one that envelops us all seasoned politicians. Only because, you have started out on the right path. The life of helping others, no better way to begin life of politics, no better way to start."

Wait a minute, they were frozen in time, what did they get into? Suddenly they all felt trapped, "what are you saying" Bosco asked? Then said: "We have no intentions of getting into politics." Patrice thinks, they feed you, think they own you. Lillianne feels happy, the thought what her husband could be. We appreciate the audience, Bosco tells the Minister, as Mande smiles embarrassed, uncomfortably. Mr Minister! As Bosco asked, he sits up on his chair, "Please tell us why we are here?"…"Me, and my family have served our people and our country. We have worked with politicians all throughout our lives, so this comes to me as no surprise."

Now he knows this is getting serious. The Minister says: "Please Chief do not get upset, this is not a trick, I just want to know if you would help."… "Respectfully Mr Minister, but first you should have asked, not raise our expectations. Here we thought, that we were going to get some funding. "Help with what" Patrice asked. "With elections, with campaigning of course". The Minister responds. "What about our work, what we started" Patrice asked. "You will get the funding." Minister said. "Once we win." Cannot believe what they are hearing, Bosco said: "Please let us think." Seasoned he is, he has dealt with politicians of all stripes. The old Chief, his father taught him well, always smile from the time you say hello, never say no. Always get back to them, insist, even if they are importunate and persist.

"Elections is fast approaching, you must tell us soon, what do you all think? We want all of you on board, not one or two but the entire crew." They were almost fooled, an attempt to be used. "What do you think? Shall we call it a day? The hotel is paid for until tomorrow, have a good rest and sleep on it. We all hope you come to the right decision, your future depends on it, ominously Mande said.

What does he mean by that? Thinks Patrice, as Mande escorts them out the door. Well, have a good evening my friends, it is approaching six PM. I will contact you tomorrow, as they hustled down the corridor. Not a word was said, as they make their way out the entrance door.

Not even a mile, they reach the hotel. Bosco says, boy I need a drink, Patrice says, as well. Lillianne looks, for the first time she agrees with him, drinking that is. I think we all do. At the hotel bar, situated at the back court yard. They all wait for their drinks, as in a race starting gun await. When the drinks arrive, they take off speaking all at once. As they all talk saying the same thing, Bosco raises his palm in front of them, he said: "It is obvious they just want to use us." Patrice agrees, so does Lillianne, what can we do she asks? As they all ask look at each other. "I do not know". Patrice would say. But do know what we cannot do. Bosco said: "We shall start there" He nods his head. Then said: "As tempting as it seems we were just given promises nothing concrete". That's true says Patrice: "They are forcing us to get involved, there is no way I can do this. It would mean the end of us, all we have built. The trust people have in us placed. They all agree, just tell them no!

Next morning first thing, a knock at the door, the small hotel room they all share, you know, revolutionaries knows quite well. Opens up to none surprise, Mande stands, dressed, crisped, he smiles. Brief case in hand a status symbol, gold buckles with trimming. "Good morning, how about breakfast." His large square black framed glasses, gives the mood trying to impress. His stature, his demeanour, his behaviour does not suit him, just outright suspicious.

A pleasant day, all Bosco would say, Mande senses the reluctance and he feels uninvited. Heaviness emits from the room, they felt betrayed for them he has failed. And in no uncertain terms, they wanted him to know this. Sorry we cannot join you for breakfast, "So you have decided, would you help us?" Yes we have Bosco said, "I cannot tell, if it is right or wrong, however, I can tell you, it goes against everything we believe in". Mande looks at Bosco, then said: "I hope you know what you're doing, I will tell my boss the Minister, but there are higher ups who would not appreciate the disrespect. Cooperate be a friend, the government, the state does not forget, who knows how this may end?"

They felt as if they have wasted time, but deep inside each swells with pride, they all now think, what perception brings. As they make their way back to the place, we have to continue, we are getting bigger by the day. So much to do, what they would not, never dare touch. Attempt to steal now they would, what we have built. The glory trust, now jealously guard with pride, real! Once imagination, once a dream, now achieved. Who knew would fight to keep? With success, comes danger replete. At their place later, not yet one week complete. Fear goading, an uneasy feeling deep inside expecting. The news come anon, reel, tears to the eyes brought, the sink feel.

Their village has been targeted by armed men in the dead of night. They loot, rape, beat, and burn what they could find, for the second time terror reigned. Chased them out, must now abandon, and brought down what they built. They are no longer protected, safe, now open game. Soldiers rogue, mercenaries, who knows? Militia they believe, they immediately think, the price they paid go against. Beaten, shaken, but none dead, seems a warning, just to threaten. Mande calls the same day, he asked: is everything okay? He confirmed their suspicion, they have now a problem. They are desperate, grabbing at anything.

Lifeline, some did throw, but no, not a chance, the Project alone would go. They would not, never would they align, do not matter the design. Would rather sink tow, now the act ruthless and low. The trust and confidence never there, imbibe the idea.

Forced to accept the concept, they are good for you, politicians sow, now disdain to show.

Patrice is now, he has always been repulsed, Bosco reassures, tells him try not to think about it. But how can he? "We will rebuild, we know how to do it. That is all they do crush, they know how to do it," Patrice said. Now, even more enraged, they cannot understand what triggered him, his reaction was apoplectic. Lillianne tries to calm him, she thinks, now the beast I see in him. Always gentle and calm, she never seen him like this.

She puts him to lie, to rest and with Bosco would discuss, they must protect him at any cost. "It was so easy for them to trigger him" Lillianne says. "He cries almost every night, for the mother he has lost, he has never vented or grieved.

One day she knew he would erupt, some they mourn and move on, for some the day never come." Patrice opens his eyes, but he heard everything they said. "Everything they take" he says. In a state, dazed like a bad dream. "They leave us with nothing." He understands, does no one else?

"You are missing everything," he tells Bosco and Lillianne.

"For some it is just a game, we live and build, they kill and break then we must pick up and build again. It does not stop, where in this cycle do we get off? I have had enough, today I tell you, at any cost will put a stop."

Patrice Continues: "I have done everything right, no matter my plight. Held the course to stay alive, constrained

242

by day worried at night. I am not the killer they wanted me to be. Turned out not, did not plunder, I did not rob. Instead, with gracious help, I educated myself. When the time came those in need I helped"..."Politicians are parasites, the lowest form of life. No one even you can tell me different, they are from us. They are poles apart, smile in your face and then stab you in the back. It is never about you, power and profiting, is what it boils down to."..."I have never met one sincere." Patrice continues: "Look around none there, demit office then saint become, preach the word of god, and for the poor protest, their cause champion."

"These politicians, why so much hate?" Lillianne asked, Patrice would say: "I just cannot tolerate, put up with their bogus showmanship. Think about all they have done. From the beginning, just worse, made no difference none.

Who would have thought possible, the destruction, the obstruction, they managed, and were very able"..."If I were to pick up a gun, I would be just like them, this I tell you what they want. They would defend, and claim the right to hold on to power until the end"..."What we must, what we should do, we know. We would deal with, whatever they may throw." The three now look at each other. They agree, they must stand up and fight, Lillianne makes the call, she said: "Patrice is right."

By this time, the other members of the team arrive. They huddle, we are strong. Thought they were part of solution, not the problem. How they were dragged in the middle of a confrontation. Already, most of the province has been covered, they have built up followers, friends and well-wishers. They have eyes everywhere, one can say, for sure they can help us, look out we need to be more vigilant and aware. Establish network insiders, those who can warn. Patrice would say:

"This is only the beginning." His fear, the worst is coming. Still coming to terms with all that is happening. A car pulls up outside, the engine revs, then dies. The local official from government walks in. The pendant shines, the silver cross on his chest, the chain that bears does well. "Good day my friends" he said, "blessings, I wish you peace, my friendship come offering." His hope, they are welcoming.

The official: "I am so sorry, I heard what happened. I want to clear the air, this was not sanctioned from by anyone from the government. It was the doing of that petty wannabe Mande, he did this personally. He promised, he said he would deliver the support of Katanga, but did not say how. I must tell you, we are not all like that. We have watched, we have observed, all that you have done and all that you have built, not wanting anything in return. I will help you with all that you need, rebuild the village, I will be there for you with all the resources, until complete." Patrice is shocked, he is sceptical, he does not believe, he says: "I would have to wait and see."

Lillianne smiles: "you see Patrice." She is still trying to convince, she wants him to know, there are many bad, but some good. She said: "You could be, one of those, you are one of them but, a shining example. You have what it takes, better the world will make. You are so young, in this short time look at all you have achieved…who knows when you reach that age, at that point, what you would have accomplished."

It is now very clear Patrice realises, Lillianne wants him to get into politics. Everything makes sense, that look in the Minister's office. The support and constant push, first Cap, then Sister Beatrix, Lillianne now, she manages. What do they know, that I do not? Patrice thinks: A sign on my forehead that readout, 'Leader in the making help out.' Flattered and honoured, but to get involved with the thing he hates the most. He is not one of them, the reluctant hero. He knows that one day he would, that only from inside, can you change things, he could.

All along listening, Bosco Proposes: "Start local take care of your people, we all know where it will get you." Patrice understood, then said: "What you say is true, our Project comes first and foremost, this we must continue. The organisation from nothing we took, where we have reached, when we look." "But it is time to think about your future, Bosco tells Patrice. Continue your work when you get in, access to resources need not go begging." Patrice replies: "You have made your point, to you I will listen, but must first wait and see what the next round shall bring."

Two thousand eighteen, election comes round again, after much speculation, what would it become? What would happen? The centre piece democracy and transition, after all they have been through. He could have fought to the last man, stand in government, relic of the past, stay and fight. To the last drop, they will suck the lifeblood. Should have never been there, for him the father paved way, somehow managed by luck and brute force. Two decades past, held on to power, it is obvious and suspicious, in him no one trusts. Not without a bang, would he go out, the last shot, denouement.

Slipping away they cannot stand it, would do everything possible to create, wait for a miracle hasten it. The force every asset released, brought in special mercenaries. Would pull tricks from every book, would revive some old. Suspend elections, prevent it ever happening. Hundreds have died, since election was announced, but the people would never give up. They would band, with the church hold hand, the U.S.

finally, would take a stand. The mass graves uncovered, the bodies of those who would stand up. Investigators summarily executed, the Nations disrespected, the sham trial put on, fools no one. Thus remains splintering, at large those perpetrated. The gauntlet run, evade sanctions, Kofi Anan's last call. Past, present, African presidents, all, warns of grave danger, beckon call.

Sit on the bench well you are not immune, will assassinate who does not rule. High tech equipment would employ, block signal emanate the voice, stifle, stop the process, those who report lack of progress. Refuse visas of international observers, create the environment and conditions, steal elections, disguised and not. Soldiers and militia they placed planned well before, in advance they anticipate. Would marched on Kasai rid pockets of resistance. Report by election shot, within the year over five thousand dead. Hundreds of schools destroyed, what troubled them? Children pay the price, the civilian movement. One and a half million displaced, thousands cross the border, they would escape, flee to Angola.

Chapter Twenty

Democracy

The forcefully displaced and the economic migrants. They have paid the ultimate price, their lives have sacrificed. All they have endured, if they do survive. Will return when it is over, home to where they belong. In another's country not theirs, in another's land they sit and long. Must go back to where they were born. Indeed, they are not alone, immigrants all around the world. Forced to migrate, forced to run, in Africa, in Asia, America and Europe, west and East, stuck at the border, they beg and plead. What to do, they came first, now the gate closed. No fault of theirs, refuge seek, settle in land not their own. Were second class, remain, now are branded and stained. Cannot fight the stigma, their children will continue to suffer. The world that we gave them, their inheritance. Take all that we could, destroy 'what' they should. To a life unpredictable, uncertain, misery hopelessness, dependency and poverty. The people, the poor children, makes no sense to them. This world inherit, they try to pick up the pieces. They will never understand, that they are the lost generation.

Do we see the problem?
Patrice asked himself and them.

This young man, all that goes through his head, frustrated most of the time, he is still trying to understand. The wavelength he must appreciate. He knows what he must do, the need to create. Where he came from, for now have reached this point. Where he is going, the many challenges, he will confront. But how to this did it come? Give thought at this point, he thinks about sometimes aloud, the thoughts arrange in his head. About the millions that suffer, not only here, but the world over. One of the lucky ones, he thinks the only one. He thanks the planets above, the stars, is it his destiny, or is it luck. Certainly, if it was?

The blessing that showers.

But most of all, understandably, importantly, he thanks the people, who supported and stood by him. Maybe someone, something guided them, by their hand, led, or by his to them, fortuitous, by luck. "I am glad they did, who knows where I would have been. This place, chaos. I would have been lost, who knows by now, dust." Patrice told himself. He thinks about, he wonders about destiny. Is it real? To go somewhere? To do something? The sense he feels, we were born to achieve. He is overwhelmed, the questions perplexed, nevertheless. The feeling, that this is so for him. How else did all this happened? His destiny, however it came, he feels calling. All are the same, he reminds himself. So maybe it is our nature, a person's character, in any event, we all know what we are after.

The election results come, would contest some, many they protest, the opposition, observers, and the church. Felix, happy the one, victorious would emerge. Some look back, some would vent, Patrice the optimist he is, all he sees is opportunity. What is wrong with them? He asked himself, cannot they see the chance finally? What for we have been waiting, take what we get, then better make it. For years we stood on the other side of the fence. The door is now open for participation, forward hence. Last it did the great spell, four decades survived, for decades died, a living hell. The road journey has brought them finally, millions has never seen, dictatorship has killed their dream.

Democracy happening, however it turns out, work behind the scenes, kill they try, they cannot, the many utmost effort. That ship has left, bound for new frontier, a new port, Patrice is sure everything would work out.

The thought in his head, never mind who says. The change long awaited, now presents itself. What to do with it? Not squander it. Gamble away on speculation, not, suspect you would, smile and nod. The short time passes, they measure, has life gotten easier? Can we predict? Could not before the future. Vast this land the best made fools, knows not what happens, from one region to the next. But carnage reigns, now heavier the toll, his predecessor now controls.

Only divisions, unity, the absence and effect, a united front could not put up, Kabilists fragment. Felix he does what is needed, the solution long before he has pleaded. The ADF they could not control, feels as if invited, the strategy some believe, perpetuate instability. Gone, but not far needs reminding, he still controls what is happening. The promise he could not keep, the other ensure incomplete. The coalition would build alliances, the wrench in the machine, the grinding halt, kill the dream. Usurp the process, welcome discord with neighbours. On their own steal the show, the generals would fail on the very first blow. The leader Felix would never be, loyal the generals remain…he.

Attacks continue, there is massacre.
Exterminate more than before.
Thrusts harder.
State forces encounter now target.
The ADF initiated, emboldened planned it.
Internal politicking drives.
The wedge that divides.
The state of affairs never derive.
The solution, the front never realise.
The divided would fall.
A house, a society, a divided country.
No resistance encounter, low esteem falter.
They cannot have.
So what to do, smother.
Counter efforts.
Save for us.
He cannot succeed, we could not.
The signs troubling.
Get out the spell, the decades.
Never give up, but fight down.
To the last drop.
To the last man.
Must grandstand.
Only that one remains.
Last one must carry on.
Going nowhere, still young.
The struggle for greatness.
If only the name, now his own.
Inherit the battle, carry on.
He would never relinquish.
In the face of failure, shame.

Like father, go down fighting.
Juxtaposition of time.
Detritus of the man.

Death, destruction, massacre undertake.
The trail would leave for all in his wake.
Hard to make sense.
What drives, relentless?
How do they think, dictators?
A different breed must be.
Selfish, cruel, takes no responsibility.
Remorse a sin, never undertake.
Futile an effort, understanding.
Others they blame replace.
One after the other with haste.
Observed self-interest?
Benevolence reserved.
What could get return?

Two thousand nineteen.
Swiftly coming to close.
Bosco, Lillianne and Patrice.
It bites, as time flies.
The others stand by.
News come from the East.
Broken and incomplete.
They plan daily.
Plainly talk among themselves.
The policy established.
The rest stay out.
Unless matter of interest.

They hear of camps created.
Two precisely.
One the side of Kabila.
And the other called Tshisekedist.
Oh boy how they share power.
Bed fellows, stranger by the hour.
Not united what will become of it?
All, they wonder.

They hear of talks breaking down.
Of people who do not belong.
Imposters, some.
The installation of loyalists.
Wary of those some oppose it.
Groups have laid down arms.
They once fought the government.
May not love this one.
But the other definitely hated.

On the fence sits another.
Await their own army create.
Confined to barracks demobilisation efforts.
What would it bring?
Forces meddling.
Funding feeding.
What is offered?
They are pleading.

Forget those in need.
They are the ones.
By their hands created division.

Sit idle, by his devil stirs, when down.

What no one want's.

So now take precedence over all.

Hope would not resort.

The fear, go back to the time.

When where once.

"This is why I do not want to get involved with politics" Patrice, looking at Lillianne saying this. His beautiful wife, the main protagonist. He continues: "They would eat me alive, I am not like them. Would not know where to start"…"Lost I will be, from beginning to end…at that dance no small fry…the lake will swallow up this tiny fish…I do not have the stomach for this…I do not have an army, the backing, very few carry me…they demand make threats because they can…who am I but a humanitarian…it's no joke, it is no laughing matter…an extraordinary peacemaker." But they instead smiled, all did, except Lillianne. "You can be so much more, can't you see this?" She said.

His presence Bosco weighs in, a figure of speech makes his. "I have heard you all, for so long, I have been listening, Patrice has already committed himself, it is his wish, we must respect, it is his matters not what we say. What we think, what we expect, it is up to him I say." Bosco's speech succinct it is, emboldens Patrice, who then proceeds with his: "I have made my decision I would finally say this I have expressed, but most not listening." Looking into her eyes saying this. "I plan to run as an independent, would not wait until the election call, the mistake they all make, I am already on the ground holding hands lifting up, what more can one want? 'If it is fine and you all agree…would start with this…the people would represent…I will start locally."

Patrice Continues: "Stabilise this region, the point of origin, lost you will be, if you take on the whole country. Most regions are not ready, here we are proven, an able body…we have shown them the rest…set the example they must follow…the commitment displayed to the many organisations and groups and to the church people…we have brought them together… we are the best in the country…an NGO, the brightest, we set the agenda, strong willed and consistent…we take on the greatest challenges…All I can say: I have learnt all I must from this."

"It is discouraging and just downright depressing." Patrice tells his now captive audience, all the reports, those who carry it, those of us who work, those that write and conduct research… Knows it has all been wasted, we try to make sense…we try to the pieces, we try to put together"…"the wanton death and destruction, just for the hell of it. A political manoeuvre, a show of hand, a gesture grand. Those they use and abuse, discard when it is over."

"Territories they take, what they claim are all in vain, they cannot hold forever…The number of victims, faceless, never see their eyes, they execute, meaningless, the commanders, the leaders, the witness, some sit far away. On the ground the soldiers, the loyalists, to please their masters they slay."

Patrice:
"What makes them different?
From some presidents.
Considered great, one might say.
What differentiates?
But the choice of weapons.
Tanks, laser guided bombs.
Smart sophisticated, special tactics.

The others hand held device.
Small and light.
How you kill, defines you.
If you are poor savagely.
If you are rich remotely.
If you can drop a bomb.
Why execute one by one?
It is what they all want.
In Africa they call us brutal.
Rivers red, hands and feet.
Blood covered.
To the west we look.
Their heads shake, some nod.
Over here we aspire.
With one bomb.
Disintegrate with fire."

Patrice, has been harbouring all along this time, aspirations of political leadership, somehow feels he was born for it, change he can the landscape, he strongly believes this. The new dispensation, what he has lived? Provides the trigger for it, he did not express this. Matters not what they said, he would know when the time is right. Think it is coming, the first sign of democracy this is only.

Would make his appearance, when he is ready. The sign he awaits, what calls upon him? Two thousand and twenty, a couple more to go, the year it all happens. What he expects, the taste he gets, we await to see. Would not bend, fall prey to elements or succumb to inducements.

What is expected of him? He will live up to, to those gone, to those still around, for his mother who looks down. Loraine would read aloud, Cap would be so proud. Lillianne would get the life dreaming about, Marcel and Dalia would join the crowd they would cheer and vote to get him there. The Sister doubt, would sit this one out. Bosco his big brother he considers, the mentor had only one other. For years guided him, astuteness and political acumen. He can now depend on the hand so strong. The chief generous helps his people, will do for him, as he stood for them.

Not a king.
But could be.
The maker of one.
The leader finally.

This book is printed on paper from sustainable sources managed under the Forest Stewardship Council (FSC) scheme.

It has been printed in the UK to reduce transportation miles and their impact upon the environment.

For every new title that Matador publishes, we plant a tree to offset CO_2, partnering with the More Trees scheme.

For more about how Matador offsets its environmental impact, see www.troubador.co.uk/about/